Chasing The Cupcake Boy

MEN OF MELBOURNE, Volume 1

Alex Leslie

Published by Alex Leslie, 2022.

CHASING THE CUPCAKE BOY

First edition. March 1, 2022.

Copyright © 2022 Alex Leslie.

ISBN: 979-8201874315

Written by Alex Leslie.

Table of Contents

To all the cupcake boys out there, waiting to be swept off their feet.

Chapter 1

ALEX MICHAELS had barely fallen asleep when he was awakened by the shrill sound of his alarm. It was six AM already and he had only had a few hours of broken sleep. His nervousness about the coming day had guaranteed a restless night. His sleep deprived mind was not ready to face the outside world. But unfortunately, he didn't have much choice in the matter.

Forced into hiding at the age of twenty-two, he had been living alone in virtual isolation for over seven years, only daring to venture outside the comfort and safety of his secluded little house, tucked away in a quiet Melbourne laneway, when absolutely necessary. Thanks to the internet, Alex could order in pretty much anything he needed, pay his bills online and even do his tax return, all without venturing outside his front door. But occasionally, circumstances required him to come out of hiding for brief periods. Today was one such occasion.

Alex had spent the last few years working from home making cupcake instructional videos on the internet, a successful home business that had amassed him an enormous online following of fans under the pseudonym 'CupcakeBoy.' Alex never showed his face in the videos. He carefully set up each shot so only his hands were visible. To maintain his anonymity, he electronically altered his voice so no one could identify him. Alex's cupcake videos were extremely popular, with many of them having gone viral across multiple social media platforms. Between the advertising revenue he earned from the videos, sales of his popular cook books, distribution deals, paid product placements and video sponsorships - Alex had ensured his financial security. Although his inheritance from his dear departed parents certainly helped him get the business off the ground, while helping to cover the cost of buying the house and going into hiding after the incident with Jack.

Jack.

Alex tried not to think about Jack. Alex had enough to worry about, without remind himself of the horrifying circumstances that led to his current living arrangements. He was safer living alone. He was safer with no one knowing where he was. His life was in danger if he didn't hide.

Stop thinking about it. You have things to do.

Alex began his rigid daily routine by checking the security monitors. He pulled the tablet computer out of the bedside table, opened the security app and reviewed the camera feeds. The motion sensors had not been triggered while he slept and everything appeared to be normal. He turned off the tablet and returned it to it's drawer.

This morning, Alex had a meeting with a major kitchenware company, Corona Industries. They had approached him through his website, offering a lucrative sponsorship deal. Alex stood to make a huge amount of money and get some new, top of the line kitchen appliances to use in his videos. Most of the details had been worked out via email, video calls and in collaboration with his lawyer, but the Corona representatives had insisted on a face-to-face meeting to sign the final contracts.

Normally, deals like this were done entirely online. Now that legal documents could be sent via email and digitally signed, face-to-face meetings weren't usually required. But Alex suspected the higher ups at Corona wanted a chance to meet the *real* CupcakeBoy, who was famously elusive and never showed his face. Alex had once been described as the Banksy of Cupcakes, a title he accepted with amusement, considering his artistic abilities definitely didn't extend beyond cupcake decorating.

But for the kind of money Corona was throwing at him, Alex could handle a quick meeting in a conference room in the city. He wasn't exactly desperate for money. Far from it. Over the last six years, CupcakeBoy had earned him a staggering amount of money. Because of his circumstances, he didn't live an extravagant lifestyle and had no reason to splash his cash around. Most of his earnings were in the bank or invested. But $50,000 plus several thousand dollars in kitchen equipment was hard to pass up. His existing kitchen appliances were starting to get to the end of their useful service life, having withstood years of punishment as Alex made his cupcake videos. The money could be invested for his retirement, so he could live comfortably in his old age.

Assuming I live that long.

Obviously, leaving the house was a huge risk, but keeping the meeting short and traveling to and from the city as quickly as possible should reduce the danger of exposure.

None of which will happen if I don't get out of bed and get ready to go!

With a resigned groan, Alex threw back the covers, reached for his walking cane – balanced between his bed and the side table – and slowly limped his way to the bathroom to clean himself up and get dressed. His back was not too sore today, but he was having some cramping in his right thigh. The symptoms of the nerve damage were often difficult to predict, and would vary wildly from day to day, even hour to hour. As he stripped off his clothes, he tried to avoid looking in the bathroom mirror. He didn't want to see the hideous scars that marred his body. He certainly didn't want to see what seven years in cupcake jail had done to his waistline. He'd never been skinny, but all these years of only being physically capable of the most minor exercise had clearly taken it's toll.

Showered, shaved and dressed in the new suit he had ordered from a Big and Tall menswear website especially for this meeting, Alex entered the kitchen, switched on the overhead light and set about organising some breakfast.

The kitchen was dominated by a huge lighting rig which hung from the ceiling, along with several camera tripods in various positions. When Alex first bought the house, the first thing to be done was have the interior completely renovated, with the kitchen a top priority.

Since the kitchen would double as a workspace for filming his cupcake videos, Alex had custom designed the kitchen to include extra large benches, a walk-in pantry, a big dining table in the centre of the room and all new stainless steel appliances. The shabby old kitchen had been totally transformed into a stylish but utilitarian space that featured clean lines and wide empty surfaces. Well, empty except for his toaster and, of course, his new coffee machine.

The fancy device, featuring a built in milk steamer and came with a big sample case of flavoured coffee pods, had arrived just last week. Alex had bought the machine online in the hopes he would be able to have real cafe-style coffee at home. But so far, he hadn't quite mastered it's operation. This morning he hoped he would have more luck. After a bit of frustration and choice words, he managed to produce a reasonable looking cup of something called 'Madagascan Mocha' and settled at the kitchen table with his Vegemite toast.

Alex had just enough time to take his morning pain medication, eat his breakfast and knock back his coffee before he would have to order his ride share and depart. He could have driven his little SUV, parked in the secure lockup garage next to his house, to this morning's meeting, but parking in the city was a nightmare, and the chances of finding a space close to where he was going were slim at best. Even with his cane and the pain meds, Alex could only walk a short distance before his spinal injury would leave him in crippling agony.

Clearing away the breakfast things, Alex double checked his messenger bag to ensure he had all the documents and presentation notes that he had printed last night, along with all the other items he would need for his excursion into the outside world. He opened the ride share app on his phone, requested a ride, and quickly checked the exterior security camera feeds to ensure it was safe, activated the alarm system, locked the front door and stepped into the courtyard in front of his house.

His little two-bedroom house, which Alex had purchased sight-unseen seven years ago when he first went into hiding, was surrounded on all sides by high concrete walls which obscured any view from the street. The space between his house and the large front wall featured a bare concrete floor, a few potted palms and an outdoor table setting that Alex enjoyed using at night when the weather was nice and the stars were bright in the sky. The only point of access to his property was via the large iron security door in the middle of the big front wall that separated the courtyard from the laneway that Alex lived on. He doubted anyone walking passed the front wall would even suspect a residential house was even there, and that's just the way he liked it.

After unlocking the heavy iron security door, stepping out into the laneway and securing the door behind him, Alex slowly limped down the lane to the street corner, where the ride share car was waiting to pick him up. The driver, a scruffy man with big bushy eyebrows and smelled vaguely of garlic, was clearly not a morning person or remotely interested in exchanging small tall. Alex did not have a problem with the lack of conversation. His own social skills were a bit rusty after so many years alone. He had forgotten the kinds of inane conversations people had in these situations, so sitting in silence was not nearly as uncomfortable as it might have been for others.

The journey to the centre of the city should only take about fifteen minutes, but a combination of rain, heavy traffic and an accident on the Westgate bridge meant the roads were gridlocked and traffic was crawling at a snail's pace. Thankfully, Alex had had the foresight to leave extra early to ensure he would arrive at the meeting with plenty of time to spare. His near-pathological hatred of being late meant he was usually ridiculously early for appointments, but the heavier than usual traffic meant he was cutting it very fine.

Only a few blocks away from his destination and with just ten minutes to spare, Alex decided it would be quicker to get out and walk the rest of the way. He asked the driver to pull over, thanked him for the ride and jumped out at the nearest cross street. Ducking under cover to escape the rain, Alex slowly began his journey up the street, passing office buildings, and saw in the distance a small cafe with tables set up on the street under large umbrellas. He recognised the cafe, *The Cuppa Hut*, from when he looked up directions online last night. The meeting was being held in the office building next door. He could already smell the heady aroma of freshly brewed coffee and buttery pastries hanging in the air. Alex had hoped to stop in at the cafe for a real cup of coffee before going into the meeting, but the heavy traffic delay had put an end to that idea. He might quickly stop in after the meeting if the cafe isn't too crowded.

Be sensible. Get in. Get Out. Go straight home. Don't take any foolish risks. Are you trying to get yourself killed?

Early morning commuters filled the footpath, jostling with each other as they all struggled to get to where they were going. A couple of times, Alex was nearly pushed over when a few clumsy pedestrians were concentrating more on their smartphones rather than what was right in front of them, but he persevered, slowly limping toward his destination. Being surrounded by so many people was distressing for Alex. Like it or not, he had become accustomed to solitude, and the crush of so many strangers was making it difficult for him to keep his eyes out for potential danger. Just as he was passing the little cafe, relieved his unexpected hike was almost at an end, Alex was suddenly knocked to the ground when a large man carrying something out of the cafe collided with him and sent him flying.

Everything was in slow motion. Hitting the pavement with a sickening thud, Alex felt pain shoot through his shoulder and down his back, his walking cane slipping from his hand and skidding across the slippery wet concrete. Alex was suddenly very cold, and could feel something wet seeping into his clothes.

Am I bleeding out? Not again. I can't go through that again.

Panic began to rise within him. He opened his eyes, and was momentarily puzzled at how everything appeared to be sideways.

Oh yeah, I'm lying on the ground.

Looking up, Alex was confronted by the image of a large, muscular man dressed in casual office attire. He was crouched in front of Alex, looking intently into his eyes.

"Are you alright, mate? I'm so sorry. I didn't see you." the mystery man said softly.

The stranger was handsome. A square jaw with a dark dusting of sculpted and trimmed five o'clock shadow; closely cropped dark hair and warm brown eyes; broad, muscular shoulders and chest, tapering down to his waist in a delicious V shape; his black trousers were tight, barely able to stretch around his powerful thighs. The man was glorious. He was also a giant klutz. Alex only had a few minutes to get into the meeting upstairs. He hoped his suit still looked okay. He looked down at himself, the contents of two very large, very cold, iced coffee drinks were spilled all down his front. A combination of whipped cream and some kind of chocolate sauce splattered all over the suit jacket.

Great. This is just perfect. I look like an ice cream factory exploded all over me. Welcome to the day from Hell.

Chapter 2

NICK HAWKE crouched down beside the stranger he'd just knocked to the ground. A round, chubby guy in a gorgeous charcoal grey suit. Well, it *was* a gorgeous suit. Now it was covered in two large Mocha Mudslides. The poor guy was an absolute mess. Nick saw the walking cane lying next to the man, who was laying on his side on the cold, wet pavement outside his favourite cafe, and his blood ran cold. The guy looked like he was in a lot of pain, but was clearly trying to hide his discomfort.

A walking cane? Oh my God, he's disabled. What the hell have I done?

"Are you hurt? Don't try to move. I'll call for an ambulance to check you out." Nick reached into his trouser pocket to grab his phone, but the man stopped him.

"No! I'm fine! Please, don't call anyone," the man sounded almost panicked.

Did he hit his head when he fell?

"I'm going to be late for my meeting. I have to go." the man winced as he tried to get up, reaching out for his cane. Nick passed it to him and tried to help him to his feet, but the stranger was having none of it.

"I'm perfectly capable. I don't need any more of your help. You've done quite enough already!" the man spat out acidly. Nick could feel his face getting hot with guilt. Whoever this guy was, he had a temper, and Nick was a little ashamed to admit that he kind of liked that. Nick took a moment to take in the man's features. He looked a little younger than Nick, maybe by a few years; his face was round and lightly flushed with sparkling sapphire blue eyes and full lips that were captivating and plump; short, chestnut brown hair, curling ever so slightly at the ends, fell in waves around his temples; his torso was difficult to judge under the suit jacket, but Nick could see a beautifully plump belly; and below that, a chunky, round ass that stuck out slightly above meaty thighs.

Nick was a self confessed chubby chaser. For as long as he could remember, he had always been attracted to *bigger-boned* guys. Just the thought of a soft, round belly or a big, juicy backside made his pulse race. Skinny guys just didn't do anything for him. He liked a bit of meat on his men. Something to hold on to. 'More cushion for the pushin' as the old saying goes. Most people, especially in the Gay community, thought it unusual that a fit, muscular, former personal trainer that worked out four or five times a week would be attracted to men who were on the heavier side. But Nick simply saw it as a case of opposites attract. His attraction to larger guys had, however, not been a smooth road for him.

Nick was a tall, handsome, muscular, slightly alpha male type, which in the Gay community meant he had his pick of all sorts of cute, twinky boys and skinny men who, in his younger days, would regularly throw themselves at him whenever he went out to the clubs. But since he wasn't interested in any of those guys, and the kind of men he *was* interested in were, more often than not, made to feel very unwelcome in the gay club scene. Internet dating was sketchy, and he had given up on that quickly. Nick had even tried going to bars and clubs that catered to bears, but found the men there, more often than not, significantly older than himself.

Not that age was an issue when it came to a casual encounter, but Nick wasn't looking for a quick fuck. He wanted a relationship. He wanted something real. It would be hard to build a solid relationship with someone if there was a large age gap. They needed to have common interests and common experiences.

So not only did Nick rarely get to meet guys that rang his bell, but Nick quickly acquired a reputation for being a 'stuck up snob' amongst the cattier queens on the scene, most of whom felt slighted by his polite rejections. This meant he too was often made to feel unwelcome when he went out for a night on the town, even to this day.

This beautiful stranger with the bluest eyes he'd ever seen was the first man in a long time that instantly struck Nick's interest. But now was not the time for cruising for cuties. The man was hurt and need to be taken care of. But the stranger was stubborn and headstrong, refusing any assistance.

"Please, let me help you up. You're obviously in pain. I feel terrible about all this. And your suit! I'm so very sorry." Nick didn't give the handsome man a chance to argue, as he carefully steadied the man under his arms and gently lifted, allowing the man to right himself at his own pace. As he helped the man up, Nick noticed a prominent but faded scar running along the top of his left hand. How had the man got such a huge scar? Now with the man standing without Nick's assistance, he was relieved to see that the stranger obviously hadn't broken any bones, but he was still concerned the man had badly injured himself.

"Please, let me take you to the hospital so you can get checked out. You may have hit your head. You might have a concussion."

"No! I'm fine. I didn't hit my head. Just landed on my shoulder hard. I've been through worse." the stranger said absently, picking up his messenger bag which had spilled it's contents in the collision.

"You should still get checked out. Better safe than sorry."

The man paused for a moment, possibly considering Nick's words. But returned to gathering the papers on the ground, most of which had been saturated by the spilled drinks. Nick hoped he hadn't destroyed anything valuable or important. By the annoyed growl emanating from the beautiful stranger, he had to assume that he most certainly had.

"I told you. I'm going to be late. I can't miss this meeting."

And with that, the stranger turned and slowly limped toward Nick's office building. Nick didn't think this man should head off on his own without at least getting checked out by a doctor, but he couldn't force the issue. Nick followed the stranger inside and joined him as he waited for the lift.

"Seriously, I'm fine. You don't have to follow me. Thanks for your help, you can go now." the man said, his eyes filled with nervous tension. Nick looked sheepishly at the man.

Boy, he's really mad at me. He'll never want to go out with me.

"Actually," he said sheepishly, "My office is in this building." Nick smiled warmly and the stranger seemed to visibly relax.

Actually I own the whole building.

Nick didn't say that thought out loud though, as he was afraid it might come across as bragging. As the owner of Australia's most popular gym chain, Hawke's Gym, Nick Hawke was a very successful man.

When he was kicked out by his God-fearing parents at sixteen after coming out of the closet, Nick was taken in by his Uncle Rob. His uncle, a life long bachelor who revelled in being the black sheep of the family, had always had a soft spot for his only nephew and welcomed Nick into his home, helped him to finish school and find his first job. Rob openly despised his sister and her husband, frequently referring to them as 'empty-headed pious morons who couldn't generate an original thought of their own if their lives depended on it,' a very colourful description that Nick had difficulty arguing with.

Starting out as a personal trainer at a little gym in Newcastle, Nick had quickly learned what made a successful gym and how to keep his clients happy. Thanks to a generous loan from his Uncle Rob when he was 25, Nick was able to purchase the little gym when the owner decided to retire. Nick rebuilt the gym from the ground up, focusing on client satisfaction and making the whole workout experience fun and friendly. Nick soon turned the business into a massive money maker. Within eighteen months, he'd opened up two more gyms, and paid his Uncle back with interest. By the age of 30, Nick owned a chain for over 100 gyms nationwide. Relocating the head office to Melbourne a few years ago, the business was going from strength to strength, branching out to new areas and would soon be expanding it's operations to New Zealand and across South East Asia.

When his uncle died last year, Nick was devastated to lose the last member of his true family. But he couldn't help but admire the old man's ability to troll his sister from beyond the grave. His uncle's will left his entire estate to his 'favourite nephew' and left his hated sister twenty dollars to 'buy rope to go hang herself' - an inheritance she elected not to claim.

As the lift doors opened and Nick and the stranger entered the car, Nick couldn't help but wish the lift would get stuck between floors. Not for creepy reasons, but it would give him more time with the cute boy with the attractive flush in his cheeks. Maybe he could even convince him that Nick wasn't the clumsy oaf he appeared to be and try to make a better impression. But the stranger hit the button for the ninth floor, which meant his time was almost up. But to Nick's alarm, he was at a loss for words. *When was the last time a guy left me tongue tied and speechless?*

When the lift reached the ninth floor, the doors slowly opened and the man attempted to make his escape. Nick, on instinct alone, placed his hand firmly on the stranger's arm, halting his movement. The man physically tensed under his touch, his breath catching. Nick wasn't sure if that reaction was a good thing or not. He stepped forward, his chest to the man's back.

"Are you sure you're okay?" Nick asked in a soft, low voice, close to the stranger's ear. The man shivered at the close contact, but quickly regained his composure. Telling Nick he was fine, the man shifted his arm which Nick instantly released. As the beautiful stranger, who's name Nick didn't even know, walked out of the lift, a business card fell out of the man's messenger bag and landed on the floor of the lift. Nick crouched down to pick it up and return it.

"Excuse me, I think you dropped this!" but it was too late. The man was gone and the lift doors closed. Looking at the card, Nick examined it carefully. Perhaps he could call the man later? Or at least learn his name. But the card was oddly generic. No phone number. No name. Just the words '*CupcakeBoy*' and a website address.

CupcakeBoy? What does that mean?

Arriving at the twenty-fourth floor, Nick stepped out of the lift and headed to his office. Outside, Andrew was at his desk engrossed in his morning email, looking slightly annoyed.

Andrew Charles had been Nick's full time personal assistant and part time driver for a few years now. Ruthlessly efficient, dedicated to getting things done and an astonishing problem solver, Nick relied on Andrew to get things done so his business could run smoothly. But over the years, Andrew and Nick had developed a fairly informal working relationship. They playfully teased each other and, at times, Nick almost felt as if *he* were the assistant, and Andrew the boss.

"You're late. And you better not have forgotten my Mocha Mudslide." Andrew murmured, not looking away from his laptop.

"Good Morning to you too! Why, yes, I *am* having a pleasant day. How about yourself?" Nick replied with enough insincere sweetness to cause a toothache.

"I haven't had my coffee yet. I'm not ready to process you're excess of personality. So? What happened to my caffeine hit?"

Nick scowled, hoping he could get Andrew to cower slightly under his imposing stare. He should have known better. Andrew just grinned at him, which made Nick burst into a boisterous laugh.

"Sorry, I did actually get us coffee. But I had a minor accident downstairs. I didn't get a chance to replace them."

Andrew's teasing comments halted immediately as he stood up, "Accident? Are you okay? Are you hurt?" concern filling his eyes.

"I'm fine. I accidentally collided with a bloke when I came out of the cafe. Ended up spilling everything all over the poor guy. Knocked him to the ground. I helped him up, and tried to get him to get checked out by a doctor, but he insisted he was fine."

Andrew visibly relaxed, his eyes filled with relief. Despite their jokes and sniping exchanges, Nick knew Andrew genuinely cared for Nick, and did everything he could to make his boss's life easier.

"Well, I'm glad you're alright."

Seeing his boss was fine, Andrew switched back to a more jovial mood, "You big lummox! I hope you got the man's details. The least you could do is offer to get his clothes cleaned. I bet he was a mess with two Mocha Mudslides all over him."

"Actually," Nick said quietly "I tried to get his details, but he was kind of pissed at me. He dashed off to the ninth floor so he wouldn't be late for a meeting."

"He works in this building?" Andrew sat back down at his desk and looked up the building directory on his laptop. "Ninth floor is 'Corona Industries' - I think they make kitchenware? Appliances. Ovens. That sort of thing. You could go down there and look for him. Apologise and offer to have his suit cleaned. Maybe even pluck up the courage to ask him out?" Andrew said the last part with a smirk. Nick blushed.

How did Andrew know I was interested in the beautiful stranger?

"Don't look so shocked! The goo-goo eyes you had when you talked about him before, I'd have to be an idiot not to notice you were obviously interested in him." Andrew smiled smugly.

"Okay, yeah, I liked him. But it doesn't matter. He was so pissed at me. He'd never agree to go out with me." Nick must have looked like a kicked puppy, because Andrew's gleeful grin faded.

"Why don't you focus on smoothing over his ruffled feathers first? Apologise. Offer to clean or replace his suit. Then, once things are a bit less crazy, you can make your move."

Nick gave Andrew's advice some serious thought. There would be no harm in going down to the ninth floor later and taking a look around.

If I could find the man, offer to clean or replace his clothes, maybe…

"I'll think about it. In the meantime, anything to report?" Nick decided a change of subject was in order.

"Your meeting with the local regional manager has been shifted to next week, so besides the usual overnight paperwork, you're free and clear today." Andrew reported, not missing a beat.

"Excellent. I'll get on with it."

Nick withdrew from Andrew's desk and proceeded into his office, glad that the conversation about his personal life was finished, or at the very least, put on hold for the time being. Nick had a feeling Andrew's curiosity would raise it's head eventually, but he had more important things to do than gossip with his assistant.

Nick sat at his desk, still clutching the mysterious business card in his hand. Curiosity got the better of him, and he opened his laptop, turned it on and typed in the website address from the card. A colourful page appeared on the screen featuring images of cupcakes. Beautiful cupcakes. Fancy cupcakes. Over the top cupcakes. Clicking on one of the cupcakes, an elegant pale yellow treat covered in delicate edible flowers, a video started playing. A man was demonstrating how to make the cupcakes and decorate them. All Nick could see was the chef's hands. His face never appeared on screen. As the chef explained the best way to make a smooth cupcake batter, Nick noticed the hand holding a large wooden spoon. That distinctive scar on the back of the hand.

It's him! It's actually him!

Nick could barely contain his excitement and his heart started pounding. But wait, the voice is wrong. The beautiful stranger's voice was slightly higher. The guy in the video spoke with a much deeper voice. Almost as if it had been changed electronically. But why would he do that? Why would he change his voice?

After going through the CupcakeBoy website and a bit of Googling, Nick realised his mystery man was apparently a very popular online cook. His website featured hundreds of cupcake tutorial videos, and according to several blogs, CupcakeBoy was notoriously secretive and never did face-to-face interviews. Nick couldn't find his real name, or even a single photograph of him. But the scar of the back of the hand left no doubt that CupcakeBoy and the handsome stranger from downstairs were one and the same.

Then it suddenly hit him. Corona Industries. They make kitchenware.

He doesn't actually work in the building.

He must be just here to meet with someone from that company! Nick launched himself out of his chair and grabbed his phone off his desk, pocketing it as he rushed out the door. If he didn't get down to the ninth floor now, he might never get the chance to see CupcakeBoy again.

Dashing passed his desk, Nick told Andrew he needed to go out, and would text him if he needed anything. Not waiting for Andrew to make any jokes at his expense, Nick ran across the floor toward the lifts and waited impatiently for the car to arrive. When the lift dinged and the doors finally opened, he burst inside, thankful the car was empty and no one else needed to get in. He punched the button for the ninth floor followed by the button to close the doors.

Please still be here. Please give me a chance.

Chapter 3

ALEX EXITED the lift as quickly as possible, dashed around the corner, burst into the men's restroom and tried to breathe. His pulse was racing and his heart was beating like a drum. How could a stranger's touch or him speaking softly in his ear provoke such a reaction? His attempts to hold onto his anger were being overwritten by his totally unexpected feelings of arousal.

But he didn't have time to analyse his conflicting emotions. His meeting with the Corona executives was due to begin any moment. He needed to try and salvage the situation and clean himself up as best he could. He moved over to the sinks, dropped his bag on the floor and looked in the mirror.

Oh my God. I look worse than I thought. This is a disaster!

Any attempt to clean himself up would be futile. His outfit was completely ruined. Worse still, the accident downstairs and caused his trousers to split down the back, leaving a very obvious hole exposing his underwear. Alex removed his suit jacket and, using paper towels from next to the sinks, did his best to remove the worst of the whipped cream and chocolate sauce, but it was hopeless. His shirt had massive dark coffee stains down the front which couldn't be dealt with in the time available. Resigned, he tied his suit jacket around his waist to cover his exposed backside, straightened his coffee soaked tie and collected his bag from the floor.

It's the best I can do. Fingers crossed they don't judge me too harshly.

Alex left the restroom and approached the reception area manned by a young woman sitting behind a large, imposing desk. She eyed him with speculative amusement.

"May I help you, sir?" she asked with insincere sweetness and an obviously fake smile.

"I'm Alexander Michaels. I have an appointment with Sandra Reynolds."

The receptionist typed on her laptop, and with an air of casual disinterest, directed him to the large conference room down the hall on his right, telling him Ms Reynolds and the team were waiting for him.

Great, I'm late and I've kept them waiting. What a perfect first impression.

Alex thanked the receptionist, who had already returned to her work, effectively dismissing him. He made his way down the narrow hallway, moving as fast as he could, and entered the large conference room.

The room was dominated by enormous floor to ceiling windows. The view of the surrounding cityscape would be spectacular if Alex had the time to stop and admire it. Inside, he found two men and a woman, all immaculately dressed in sharp business suits that were not soaked in iced coffee drinks. The executives were sitting on one side of a long, polished wood conference table. They looked up as Alex entered, the expressions on their faces neutral, but morphing into looks of confusion as they took in his bizarre appearance.

"I'm so sorry I'm late. I'm Alexander Michaels. I had a little accident downstairs." his feeble attempt to explain himself apparently not going down well with the impatient executives.

"Please, take a seat. Let's get this over with." the sharply dressed woman said, whom Alex presumed was Ms Reynolds since no introductions were made. She also made no attempt to disguise her annoyance at either Alex's appearance or tardiness. Probably both.

This is mortifying. Get it together Alex! You can do this!

He took his seat opposite the executives, wincing as he sat. Alex would be in a great deal of pain later when the bruising started to take hold. But for now, he would have to push through his discomfort and get the job done.

"Mr Michaels, before we get to the signing of the contracts, we understand you have prepared a presentation about your business." one of the male executives said, using air quotes when he said the word *business*.

Alex had a bad feeling about this. In all their previous communications, the Corona representatives had been nothing but positive and even excited about this deal. But sitting here now, these people seemed bored, disinterested and borderline hostile. Clearly, he had made a very bad first impression. But the situation could still be turned around. He reached into his messenger bag to remove his notes and printed handouts, but the paperwork was ruined. As he pulled the dripping sheets of paper out, the executives openly rolled their eyes, their faces set in obvious displeasure.

I think this deal is dead in the water. These people are never going to take a fat guy covered in coffee seriously.

"Look, it's clear you're not ready to present your proposal," Ms Reynolds said and, with a none to subtle edge of condescension, continued, "Perhaps, when you've had a bit more experience in the business world, we might be able to work something out. Until then, we'll keep an eye on you and be in touch."

With that, the three executives stood, the universally acknowledged sign for 'end of meeting' or, more bluntly, 'get out.' Alex shoved the ruined paperwork back in his bag, meekly thanked the three executives for their time, and told them he looked forward to hearing from them. He knew full well he would never hear from any of them ever again. He rose from his chair, and made his way to the door. As he walked down the hallway towards the reception area, he could hear the executives burst out laughing and openly mock him.

Alex had never been so humiliated. He'd worked hard on this deal. He'd worked hard on his presentation. It was totally unfair how this deal had been so completely wrecked through no fault of his own. The thought then occurred to Alex that those people never even bothered to ask if he was alright after he mentioned having been involved in an accident downstairs. The mocking and laughter was the most unprofessional behaviour Alex had ever encountered in all his working life. If this is how they treated a potential business partner, then perhaps he should be glad he wasn't going into business with Corona Industries. CupcakeBoy was doing well financially, and Alex was constantly being contacted by brands begging to do business with him. Corona Industries was no big loss.

I could have used that money though. It would have gone a long way to shoring up my retirement fund.

There was nothing more to be done now. There would be other deals. Right now, Alex just wanted to get out of here, go home and wash away this terrible day. A long soak in his big spa bath would rinse away the coffee and soothe his now seriously aching muscles. Alex tried to let go of his anger and humiliation, but until he was safe and secure back in his little house, he would just have to deal with the built up tension that was doing his injuries no favours.

But any chance of a quick getaway was quickly scuttled as he approached the lifts. There, standing in the reception area, was the handsome coffee klutz. He looked towards Alex and smiled warmly.

Oh, what the hell does he want now?

Chapter 4

NICK EXITED the lift on the ninth floor and approached the Corona Industries reception area. A woman sitting behind the large reception desk looked up from her laptop, her eyes went as large as saucers when Nick smiled at her. She blushed and smiled widely in return.

"Good Morning, sir. How may I be of assistance?" the receptionist gushed.

"I hope you can help me. I'm looking for a man who came in here sometime in the last half hour or so. You wouldn't have missed him. His clothes had been ruined." Nick lowered his voice for the last part, not wanting to draw too much attention to his mystery man's attire.

The receptionist's smile faltered slightly, possibly unhappy that Nick had not come down to the ninth floor in search of *her.*

"Yes, he came in a little while ago. He's in a meeting down in the conference room. I'm not sure how long he'll be, but you're welcome to take a seat and wait if you like." she pointed to the waiting area.

Nick surveyed the row of cheap, uncomfortable-looking plastic chairs that ran along the wall. Nick always thought you could tell a lot about a business by how they treat their customers and clients. Corona Industries' ugly, budget-priced reception furniture spoke volumes. Nick's offices had comfortable leather chairs in the reception area. They cost more, but made a much better first impression. Corona clearly wasn't that worried about making good first impressions.

Nick was about to take a seat when some loud laughter, which carried down from the long hallway beyond the reception desk, caught his attention. There was CupcakeBoy. The man he had been looking for was slowly limping his way up the hallway. His face was red and his eyes cast downward. His suit jacket was tied around his waist and his shirt and tie were heavily stained from the earlier disastrous encounter downstairs.

I found him! I actually found him! But he looks so upset. Is this my fault?

The man looked up as he approached the reception desk, and his clear sapphire eyes locked on to Nick. He visibly started and looked genuinely upset. Nick stepped forward, a friendly smile on his face.

"I'm so glad I found you. Are you okay?" Nick was concerned the man's flushed face was a symptom of being is pain from the collision.

"Am I okay? Seriously? Well, let's see," the man squared his shoulders, clearly ready for a fight, "First, my new suit is ruined; I get knocked to the ground and hurt my shoulder; my pants are split so my whole backside is showing; I just lost out on a business deal worth tens of thousands of dollars because I look like I've been molested by a chocolate sundae and my back is throbbing like an absolute bitch! Am I okay? Oh, I'm just peachy! Thanks for asking!" the man spat out with as much venom as he could muster. He barged past Nick and hit the call button for the lift.

"I'm so sorry about everything," Nick said sheepishly, "This is all my fault. Please accept my sincerest apologies and allow me to try and make it up to you. I really feel terrible about everything." Nick hoped he wasn't coming on too strong, but he really needed this man to understand he was serious about making amends. The lift dinged and the doors slid open. Nick and the man entered the car, the man pressing the button for the ground floor. CupcakeBoy sighed, his angry face softening. His shoulders sank and the fight appeared to drain right out of him.

"Apology accepted," he said softly, "I guess I'm sorry too. I don't usually get this angry, but things... things have just been a total disaster today. I didn't mean to lash out like that back there," the man looked genuinely ashamed of his outburst, "I'm not used to being around other people, and my social skills are a little rusty."

Nick was curious as to why this man didn't spend much time around other people, but was so ecstatic that he had finally been forgiven, he let the man's confession slip by without further comment.

"Thank you. I want to make this up to you. For starters, I'm replacing your suit. I can't believe how clumsy I was down at the cafe. I promise I'm not the big lummox you probably think I am," Nick tried for a little subtle flirting, "I've never literally swept a man off his feet before." he said with a chuckle.

Okay, that was a cheesy line. But a bit of innocent flirting couldn't make things worse.

The man blushed but rolled his eyes. He obviously thought the line was cheesy too, but his lips curled slightly in the faintest outline of a smile. He wasn't offended. Perhaps Nick was in with a chance after all?

"I never called you a lummox. But you certainly are big. Not that I can talk! But I'm not exactly the same kind of big. But obviously, you know that." the man was rambling nervously and looked down at his feet, taking a few shaky breaths.

The lift doors opened and they stepped out into the ground floor lobby area. The stranger with the blushing smile pulled his phone out of his messenger bag, but his face fell when he saw the screen was smashed, dripping with coffee. The device was completely dead.

"So much for ordering a ride share," the man muttered and looked out the glass doors ahead, "Oh good, and it's still raining! That'll make it easy to get a taxi." he said with undisguised sarcasm.

Nick whipped out his own phone and texted Andrew, asking him to bring his car around to the front of the building immediately. Andrew texted back seconds later saying he would be there in five minutes.

"Please, let me take you home. My car is being brought around as we speak. It's the least I can do after everything." Nick looked into the man's beautiful eyes with a hopeful gaze, willing the stranger to agree.

"You don't have to do that. I'll just walk until I can find a taxi," the man said, but with little confidence in his voice. "Besides, don't you have to get back to work? Won't your boss get angry with you if you just take off in the middle of the working day?"

"Nah! I *am* the boss. And I'm sure my employees can live without me for a while," Nick smiled warmly, "Regardless, I'd never forgive myself if I let you wander off in this weather alone and something happened to you. Please, let me take you home."

As if on cue, Nick's big black Audi Q7 pulled up in front of the building. Nick placed his hand on the back of the man's neck to gently guide him out to the car. The man startled briefly, but relaxed into the soft touch. He opened the rear passenger door and helped the man inside, then slid in beside him.

"After all that's happened today, I still don't know your name." Nick said as he clicked on his seatbelt. The man seemed to hesitate, but after a moment he shrugged absently.

"Alex, my name is Alex."

"Nice to meet you, Alex. I'm Nicolas Hawke, but everyone just calls me Nick." he extended his hand to Alex and they shook hands. The instant their hands clasped, it was like a surge of electricity passed through them. Nick's heart started beating wildly, and if the shy eyes and blushing cheeks on Alex were any indication, he was similarly affected.

"What's your address, Alex? Not that sitting on the side of the road with you isn't fun, but I think we should get you home so you can clean up and change out of those clothes I ruined." Nick said, trying to be lighthearted. Alex hesitated again.

Why does he keep doing that? He looks almost scared. Am I that intimidating?

But he quickly rattled off his address. The privacy screen was up, so Nick pressed the intercom and recited Alex's address to Andrew. The car pulled into traffic and the car sped through the rainy streets of the city toward Alex's home.

"Big fancy car with a driver? Must be nice." Alex remarked quietly as he looked around the plush interior of Nick's Q7.

"Yeah, I resisted getting something fancy for ages. But when my banged up old Commodore VY finally gave up the ghost, I fell in love with this gorgeous girl."

Nick loved his car. He loved driving even more. The Q7 was a dream to drive, comfortable enough for everyday city driving or going out on the open road.

"I don't get to drive it as much as I'd like too, but when I do have a bit of free time, a nice, long, relaxing drive up the coast roads is a great way to spend the weekend." That gave Nick an idea.

"Hey, you should come along with me some time. We could make a day of it. Go see The Twelve Apostles, pack a picnic lunch. It'd be great." Nick was hopeful Alex would love his idea and agree to come with him. They could go this weekend and get to know each other better.

Alex seemed to stiffen at the suggestion. He began fidgeting with his fingers and looked down at his hands.

"That's probably not a good idea." he said, his voice barely a whisper. Nick was disappointed at the refusal.

Maybe he doesn't like me after all. Or maybe I'm going to fast for him. I shouldn't be so pushy.

The car turned into a short, narrow laneway, barely wide enough for the SUV to navigate. About halfway down, they pulled up outside a tall cement wall. It must be at least three metres high. The wall was dominated by a large iron door, and further along the lane, a secure garage roller door.

"This is me. Thanks for the lift. I'm sorry to have taken you so far out of your way." Alex quickly mumbled, as if he were desperate to get away. The rain was still coming down heavily.

"No problem. Like I said, it was the least I could do after ruining your day so spectacularly." Nick picked up Alex's messenger bag from the floor, opened the passenger door and jumped out, holding the door open for Alex as he exited the vehicle. He dashed across to the large iron door and tried to unlock it as quickly as possible so he could get out of the rain. Nick followed him into a small courtyard and walked toward a cozy little house, completely hidden from the street by the dominating walls that surrounded it. He noticed barbed wire on the top of the walls, and several security cameras in strategic positions around the courtyard and on the house's small front porch. The windows on the house all had large metal security bars.

It's like a fortress. Why is Alex living in a prison?

Nick remembered he was still carrying Alex's messenger bag. He handed it to Alex as the man unlocked the front door. He turned and nervously thanked Nick again for driving him home.

"You're very welcome. It was my pleasure. Oh, that reminds me!" Nick fumbled in his pocket and pulled out the business card, "You dropped this in the lift this morning. I wanted to return it to you, Cupcake Boy," he said with a smile and a wink.

Alex paled. He dropped his bag just inside the door with a clatter and stumbled back. He looked visibly shaken. "I don't know what you're talking about. That's not mine!" he said abruptly, panic painted across his face and slammed the door shut.

What the hell? What just happened?

Nick knocked on the door but got no reply. He heard beeping sounds coming from just inside the door. An alarm system, perhaps?

What did Nick do wrong? And why did Alex deny it was his business card. It fell out of his bag. Nick had checked out the website, and he knew from the videos that Alex *was* CupcakeBoy, but why would he deny it? And why did he look so scared?

Man, I've really blown this. But nothing about this situation makes any sense.

Nick tried to get Alex to answer the door, but after a minute or so, he knew he was wasting his time. With a sigh, he turned away from the strange little house and dashed back into the rain. He jumped back into the car, and asked Andrew to take him back to the office.

Chapter 5

ALEX OBSERVED the outside security camera feeds until Nick returned to his car and drove away. He let out a breath he hadn't realised he was holding on to, and tried to quell the rising panic.

He knows who I am. He knows where I live. What the hell am I going to do?

The instant he saw the business card in Nick's hand, Alex had realised just how enormous a mistake he had made by leaving the safety and security of his house. He had exposed himself, in more ways than one, endangered his life and all for the sake of a signing a deal he didn't really need and ultimately failed to secure.

Those stupid business cards!

Alex had been convinced by his book publisher to have them made up as part of a subtle marketing campaign. Although Alex rarely left the house, the few times he did, the publisher suggested he could leave a few business cards with his website address on them in public places. At cafes, libraries, information desks etc. Alex thought it was stupid, but it was easier to agree than argue about it endlessly. Now he wished he'd argued a bit more. The bastard things had led to him being exposed.

For the moment, there was nothing he could do about it, so Alex focused on problems he could deal with. Namely, removing his ruined clothes and cleaning himself up. He went into the kitchen, pulled out a large garbage bag from his well-stocked utility drawer and quickly stripped off his soiled garments. There was no saving them, and he certainly wasn't going to go out to find a dry cleaner. He stuffed them into the garbage bag, along with the coffee-soaked contents of his messenger bag. The bag itself was badly stained inside and out, but he would try to clean it later. If worst came worst, it wasn't expensive, and a replacement could easily be ordered. Alex tied up the handles tightly, then placed the filled garbage bag by the front door, ready to dispose of in the outside bin when the rain finally deigned to ease off.

When Alex stepped into the hot, steamy shower in the main bathroom, all the accrued tension from the day began to slowly melt away along with the coffee, chocolate and whipped cream that had been unceremoniously dumped on him earlier. He was going to fill the spa bath and have a nice long soak, but right now he just wanted to be clean. The lavender scented body wash which, according to the website he'd purchased it from, was famous for it's relaxing and calming effects, eased the stress and tightness from his aching muscles and did wonders for his mood.

Once his hair was thoroughly shampooed, conditioned, and rinsed until squeaky clean, Alex stepped out of the shower, wrapped himself in an extra large, super soft, fluffy white towel and headed for his bedroom to get dressed. He found some old sweatpants and a battered old t shirt. They were hardly the most glamorous clothes, but they were comforting. And it wasn't like he wasn't looking to impress anyone.

After hanging the towel back up in the bathroom, Alex withdrew to the kitchen, heated up a couple of wheat heat packs in the microwave, made himself a passable cup of coffee from the frustrating new machine and settled in the living room with his laptop.

Once he found a comfortable position on the couch, the heat packs in place on his aching shoulder, Alex sipped his coffee and tried to relax. But his encounters with the mysterious Nick Hawke still weighed heavily on his mind. Nick, who barged into him and ruined his suit. Nick, who came looking for him to apologise and make amends. Nick, who made his whole body tingle with just a few breathy words in his ear.

Stop it! Don't be ridiculous! As if someone like him would be interested in a mess like me!

But Alex couldn't stop thinking about how much Nick tried to engage with him. Most guys would have gruffly apologised, or even blamed the other person for *their* clumsiness. But Nick was different. Nick went out of his was to convey his regrets. He wasn't afraid to claim responsibility for his own actions. He even drove Alex home and offered to take Alex on a picnic date. Why would he do that?

The business card.

He knows who I am. He knows I'm CupcakeBoy. And now he knows where I live.

But wait, Alex didn't need to panic. It's not like Alex will be going to that office building ever again. Realistically, Nick and Alex had no logical reason to see each other again. It's not like Nick would have any reason to come back here. Alex could relax, safe in the knowledge his secrets remained his own. It'll all be fine.

But the thought of never seeing Nick again made Alex feel oddly sad, even disappointed. Nick was so handsome. Actually he was the most astonishingly gorgeous man Alex had ever seen. Just the thought of Nick's wide, muscular shoulders, large chest, slender waist and meaty thighs had Alex's cock twitching. That thick, glossy black hair. His square, masculine jaw with it's dark day old stubble. Those gorgeous, dark brown eyes, like two pools of warm melted chocolate, and that smile that could almost cure a rainy day.

Alex closed his eyes, and allowed his hand to drift down his belly and beneath his sweatpants, lightly stroking his hardening shaft.

Okay, this is ridiculous! I'm fantasising about the man who wrecked my life today!

But Alex knew in his heart that that wasn't true. Nick hadn't ruined his life. Dramatic much? Everything that happened this morning was a simple accident. It's not like Nick knocked him over on purpose. There wasn't the slightest malice in his actions or his words. And it was really unfair of Alex to be venting his anger on this innocent stranger who really didn't deserve it. He was just using Nick as a convenient target to release his pent up rage about... other things.

Don't think about Jack. Think about something else.

Alex let his mind drift from that disturbing thought, and back to Nick in the lift. Nick standing behind him, his hard, powerful chest to

Alex's back. Leaning in and whispering in his ear. This time, Nick was muttering all sorts of erotic words, provoking that same shiver that ran down Alex's spine, warming his body and curling his toes as his heart beat faster.

Alex was stroking his cock faster and faster, moaning as he bit his bottom lip to stop himself from screaming out Nick's name. His balls tightened and he suddenly felt that familiar tingling at the base of his spine, his orgasm rapidly approaching him. His breath was short and his nerves were firing like electricity passing through his body. His sensitised body arched up and found it's release. Alex saw stars explode behind his tightly closed eyes, riding the waves of his post orgasmic pleasure.

Once he'd had a chance to catch his breath and his heart rate returned to normal, he cleaned himself up as best he could using the box of tissues on the coffee table.

What he'd just experienced was the best he could hope for from Nick. A beautiful fantasy, but nothing more. Being realistic, Alex could never have any kind of relationship with Nick. Alex wouldn't put himself in that position again. Once was enough, and that experience more than proved to Alex that anything even remotely approaching romance wasn't worth the inevitable pain and suffering.

Not that Nick would even be interested in him anyway. Big, handsome muscle men didn't go for damaged goods like Alex. And fat cripples with scars never get happy endings, if soppy Hollywood movies were to be believed.

Alex decided to just forget about today. Forget about Nick. Focus on his work. Focus on cupcakes. Focus on staying hidden. Focus on staying safe. This was what was important.

Psychos can't hurt what they can't find.

Alex spent the rest of the day relaxing on the couch. He ordered his replacement phone online and worked on the manuscript for his latest cookbook when he felt up to it. After a few hours, the pain from that morning's accident slowly started to fade. After a simple lunch of Soup, toast and a remarkably good cup of coffee, which he proudly made with little trouble from the devil coffee machine, Alex set about tidying the house and loading the washing machine in the small laundry room at the back of the house. He tried to clean the soiled messenger bag, but the inner lining was a lost cause. He placed it on top of the garbage bag by the front door, and finished up his housekeeping by wiping down the kitchen counters.

At about five thirty that evening, Alex was back on the couch, going through his Netflix watch list, trying to find something comforting to watch, when the dominating silence of the house was broken with a sharp knock on the front door.

Who could that be? Grocery delivery? They aren't supposed to be here until tomorrow.

Alex made his way to the security panel by the front door and checked the exterior cameras. In his haste to get out of the rain earlier, and obviously distracted by Nick's presence, he'd foolishly forgotten to close and lock the large iron door leading into the courtyard. A figure stood on the front porch, looking directly at the camera above the door. Alex couldn't believe his eyes. It's was Nick, smiling a warm smile, holding what looked like a cardboard box tied up with string.

What the hell is he doing back here?

Chapter 6

NICK HAD never felt this nervous before. Standing on Alex's front porch, clutching his feeble offering of freshly baked brownies from his favourite bakery, he hoped this little peace offering would be enough to get Alex to at least talk to him.

He knocked on the door and waited. He heard movement from within the house, so he knew Alex was home. But his knock went unanswered. He could hear Alex behind the door. Was he scared? Was he trying to decide if he should open the door? Then Nick remembered the security cameras. He would bet good money Alex was watching him right now. Sizing him up. Trying to figure out what to do.

Nick turned to the camera above the front door, looking directly at it. He smiled brightly, hoping to show Alex he wasn't a threat and that Nick was just being friendly.

Just as he was starting to lose hope of ever laying eyes on the beautiful boy with the gorgeous sapphire eyes, the front door opened a crack. Alex peered out speculatively, worry clearly painted across his face.

"What are you doing here? What do you want?" he said softly, his confusion at Nick's return clear in his nervous voice.

"I wanted to make sure you were alright," Nick began. "You seemed upset earlier, and I wasn't sure what I said or did to scare you, but I just wanted to let you know that you don't have to be scared of me. I just want to get to know you better." Alex, still peeping through the crack, looked sceptically at Nick for a moment, but his face softened ever so slightly, and he opened the door a little more.

"I brought you some delicious brownies from this little bakery in the city. It's my favourite place to go when I need a naughty little treat, and I thought you might like them."

"I don't think this is a good idea." Alex said, his voice wavering, his words lacking the conviction he probably wished they had.

"Brownies are *always* a good idea." Nick chuckled and held the box up in Alex's direction. Alex, still looking slightly skeptical, opened the door slightly more and accepted the bakery. He took a moment to sniff the rich chocolate scent emanating from the box, his eyes slipping closed as he inhaled the dark aroma. Nick's cock twitched at Alex's sensual reaction and stifled a groan of pleasure.

"Thank you. This is very kind of you. You didn't have to do this." Alex opened his eyes, and his face seemed to relax. Nick hoped this was a sign that Alex was beginning to trust him.

"I also wanted to ask you something. Would you join me for dinner tonight?" Nick was a bundle of nerves as he awaited Alex's response.

Please say yes! Please say yes!

"Why?" Alex blurted out, his face a study of genuine confusion and puzzlement. Nick wasn't expecting that reaction.

Had no one ever asked Alex out on a date before?

"Because I'm hungry, and I thought you might be hungry too."

Alex cocked an eyebrow at Nick, clearly not buying this explanation. Nick decided to go for broke, "I like you, Alex. I want to get to know you better. You're sexy, and you have the most beautiful eyes I've ever seen. Ever since we met this morning, I can't stop thinking about you. Please. Please, come to dinner."

Alex appeared dumbstruck. He watched Nick silently, his face changing from shocked, to skeptical, to confused, to blushingly shy. Nick could see the cogs turning, trying to make a decision, and it was the most adorable thing he had ever seen.

"Okay. I'll have dinner with you. I need to get ready." and with that, Alex closed the door and disappeared into the house. Nick was both elated and totally confused. This boy would keep him on his toes! He guessed when Alex had said earlier that his social skills were rusty, it was a serious understatement. Alex didn't even invite his date into his home while he got ready. But Nick could forgive this strange behaviour. Alex had agreed to have dinner with him. Inside, he was cheering victoriously.

Despite all his hopes, Nick hadn't been convinced that Alex would agree to have dinner with him. Coming to see Alex was a spur of the moment decision, and so he hadn't really thought ahead to what they would do if Alex actually said yes. Nick quickly tried to decide on where to take Alex on their date. Somewhere relaxed, quiet and informal, where they would be free to talk and get to know each other. He remembered the steakhouse not far from his home. It would be the perfect venue for a first date. He quickly pulled out his phone, called the restaurant to reserve a private table. It was apparently a quiet night, so the steakhouse just told him to show up whenever they were ready to eat.

Alex opened the door a few minutes later and stepped out onto the porch. He was wearing a pair of neat chinos and a dark polo top. In one hand was his walking cane, the other a chunky set of house keys.

"Will this do? I wasn't sure what to wear. I don't get out much." Alex said, looking embarrassed and shy.

"You look great, Alex," Nick assured his date, "We're going to a steakhouse, so it's very relaxed and casual. You're not a vegetarian or anything are you? I probably should have asked."

Alex shot him a quizzical look, "No, not a vegetarian. You don't get this fat eating salads," he giggled softly.

Nick was relieved. Normally, he would have checked something like that beforehand, but something about Alex scattered his brain. He'd never felt this out of sorts with a man before.

"Well, you're going to love this place. The food is excellent, it's relaxed and comfortable, and the desserts are to die for."

Alex turned, closing and locking the front door, then lead the way through the courtyard toward the large iron door. Nick walked out into the lane and unlocked the Q7 as Alex secured the iron door.

Nick held the front passenger door open for his date, and Alex carefully got in and secured his seatbelt. When Nick jumped in and closed his own door, Alex smirked at him, "No driver tonight?"

"My assistant only drives during business hours, in case I need to work or take calls while I'm on the road. I promise I'm a good driver, I hardly ever crash." he said, trying to hold a straight face, then burst out laughing.

"No, from my experience, your weapon of choice is a well aimed frozen coffee drink." Alex shot back, a big cheeky grin on his face.

"Whoa! Cheap shot! I think I'm going to have to keep an eye on you! You're very feisty tonight." Nick smiled wide, loving the playful teasing.

The rain had eased off to a mild sprinkle, and while the traffic was heavy this evening, the journey to the restaurant was quick and uneventful.

'Grillers in the Mist' - despite it's terrible pun name and neon window signage depicting a gorilla wearing a chef's hat, was actually a cosy, comfortable restaurant with a relaxed vibe and friendly staff. Having secured a parking space right at the door, Nick escorted Alex inside and they were greeted by Mindy, the teenage hostess who always seemed to be on shift whenever Nick came in.

"Welcome back, Mr Hawke! It's so good to see you again. Please, come with me. We have a lovely table prepared for you and your date." she said, grabbing two menus and walking ahead of them to the back of the restaurant. She led them to a private table in the corner. The restaurant was indeed quiet tonight, with only a small number of people scattered throughout the dining room. Nick suspected the rain had put people off, and they were all staying home in case the torrential weather started up again.

Nick pulled out a chair for Alex, and his date sat down gingerly. Nick pushed the chair in slightly, then sat down opposite. The hostess handed them a menu each, then withdrew to get water and glasses.

"Are you feeling alright after this morning's... um... excitement? I hope you aren't in any pain." Nick enquired.

"Just a little tender. A bit of bruising. Nothing I can't handle. I've certainly dealt with worse." Alex replied quietly.

That was the second time Alex had made such a comment, and Nick wasn't sure what to make of it, but decided now wasn't the time to delve, and opened his menu. Alex did the same, studying the menu carefully.

The hostess returned with glasses and a pitcher of iced water, then departed after she informed them their waiter would be with them shortly to take their order.

"What are you in the mood for? Everything here is so good." Nick asked, still looking at the menu.

"I'm not sure. I don't think I've ever been to a steakhouse before. I don't really know where to begin."

Nick raised his eyebrows at Alex's confession. He'd never been to a steakhouse before? Maybe he *was* a Vegetarian. Maybe he was just too shy to admit it? No, that doesn't make sense. Vegetarians never shut up about being Vegetarians.

"If you like, I could order for both of us. If you trust my judgement." Nick looked up from his menu and stared into his date's beautiful eyes.

"Sure, I trust you." Alex said, looking a little nervous. Despite only talking about ordering food, Nick felt insanely happy to hear Alex say that he trusted him. It felt like progress, or perhaps an omen of good things to come.

When the waiter approached, he took their drink orders, then Nick ordered two large ribeye steaks, both medium rare, with red wine sauce and big baked potatoes. He also ordered a large garden salad to share and some crusty garlic ciabatta bread for starters. The waiter relieved them of their menus and left to place their order. Nick smiled at Alex, rubbing his belly, "I haven't had a chance to eat much today, so I'm looking forward to this."

"Me too. I haven't had a steak in a very long time. The red wine sauce sounds nice."

"You keep making comments about not having done things for a long time, why is that?" Nick was dying of curiosity.

Alex considered his response carefully, then simply said, "I don't get out much these days."

"Because of your leg?"

"Um, sort of. Although my leg isn't actually hurt. I have... a spinal injury. Sometimes my legs go numb and I need the cane to keep balanced."

The waiter returned with the garlic bread. The smell of the freshly baked bread was mouth watering.

"Were you in an accident?" Nick knew he was pushing it, but he couldn't help delving into the mystery that was Alex.

"Um, sort of. I... certainly made a mistake." Alex said cryptically, but didn't elaborate. He looked distinctly uncomfortable at this line of questioning, so Nick decided to back off.

"Well, I checked out your website. Your cupcakes are amazing. How long have your been making your videos?" Nick hoped this was a safer topic.

"A few years." Alex replied, his face neutral, as if he were trying to hide what he was thinking.

"Do you enjoy it? Making cupcake videos?" Nick tried to draw Alex out, figuring a subject close to his heart would help to break the ice.

"Okay, let's cut to the chase shall we?" Alex's voice was suddenly stiff and determined, "How much?"

"Huh? I... I don't understand." Nick was puzzled by Alex's outburst, particularly the sharpness of his words.

"Of course you don't. Look, I'm not an idiot. You've brought me to this quiet restaurant, you're asking all these questions about me. Trying to get me to confess to who I really am. Are you wearing a wire? Some kind of secret video camera? Are you a journalist? Or some two-bit blogger trying to make a name for himself exposing the secret identity of the famously reclusive cupcake guy? You obviously know who I am. So, how much to keep you quiet?"

Nick was incredulous, "You think I'm trying to blackmail you?" He couldn't believe what he was hearing.

"What else are we doing here? Why else would you ask me out? You've figured out who I am. So let's stop playing games and tell me what you want." Alex said with resignation, his earlier flash of anger draining away, leaving his face pale and crestfallen.

"You've got it all wrong, I swear. All I wanted to do was get to know you. I wouldn't ask you out under false pretences. I certainly wouldn't blackmail you."

Alex's looked deep into Nick's eyes, obviously recognising the sincerity in his words. He lowered his head and blushed dark with shame.

"I'm sorry. I'm so sorry. You really just wanted to get to know me? Really? God, I feel like such a bastard. I guess I'm just so used to people being... I shouldn't have assumed... I'm sorry." Alex raised his head slightly, a single tear falling down his cheek.

"Hey. Hey, don't cry," Nick said softly, leaning forward and wiping the tear away with his thumb. Alex drew in a sharp breath at the brief contact, "Sounds to me like you have your reasons to be distrustful. But I promise, I would never do anything to hurt you. I really do like you, Alex. I think you are amazing. You're sweet, and funny, and sexy as hell, and if you'd let me, I'd really like to spend tonight proving to you how much I like you."

Nick placed a finger under Alex's chin up and nudged it up slightly, forcing Alex to make eye contact. He smiled warmly, and Alex returned the smile.

"I'm sorry I'm such a mess," Alex said as he dried his eyes, "God knows what you must think of me." Alex whispered.

"Weren't you listening? Sweet, funny, sexy as hell. And I look forward to getting to know you a whole lot better. Now have some of this garlic bread while it's still hot. I can't resist it anymore."

Nick broke off a piece of the hot, steaming bread and held the it up to Alex's lips. He opened his mouth, accepted the piping hot morsel, and groaned with pleasure. Nick's cock stiffened in response, and he stifled a groan of his own. Thank God the napkin in his lap prevented anyone from seeing what was going on down there.

"It's delicious. The garlic butter is just right, and the bread is heavenly." Alex crooned, taking the rest of the piece of bread from Nick. Nick took a bite of the bread himself and agreed wholeheartedly.

Later in the evening, after having polished off their steaks and salad, both men were stuffed. Nick asked if Alex would like to look at the dessert menu.

"Oh, I couldn't eat another thing. That steak was huge! And those baked potatoes were amazing." Alex smiled wide. He was finally looking relaxed and had apparently enjoyed himself this evening.

Nick called for the check and finished his glass of iced tea before pulling out his credit card. But Alex tried to stop him.

"Wait, I should pay for half. Let me get my wallet out." he said as he started fumbling in his pocket.

"Absolutely not. After everything that happened this morning, the least I can do is pick up the tab for dinner. Besides, I invited you out." Nick reasoned, and waved away any suggestion of Alex paying for anything. Nick had a feeling Alex needed someone to take care of him; someone to shower him with affection and to make him feel adored. Nick liked the idea of this a lot.

Alex seemed very reluctant to let Nick foot the bill for dinner, but politely thanked him and put his wallet away. Once the bill was settled, Nick stood and escorted Alex back to the car, ensuring he was comfortably seated and his seat belt on before closing the passenger door and crossing to the driver's side. He started the engine and pulled out into the evening traffic. The rain was coming down heavier again, but it wasn't nearly as bad as it had been earlier in the day. Just a mild evening shower as they zipped through the streets toward Alex's home. When they got there, Nick leapt out of the vehicle to open Alex's door, noting the laneway had no streetlights and was very dark, and escorted his date to his front door.

"Thank you for coming out with me tonight. I had a wonderful time. I'd love to take you out for dinner again soon."

Alex looked at Nick with lost eyes. He was clearly not sure what to say, or possibly trying to come to a decision.

'I'm sorry. I'm really busy at the moment, and I'm sure you are too. Plus, I'm not sure this is really a good idea. Perhaps you should try and find someone who less of a mess..."

Nick cut off Alex's rambling excuses by pressing their lips together. Alex stiffened at first, clearly shocked by the sudden intimate contact, but soon melted into Nick's embrace, whimpering slightly as Nick's tongue gently ran along his lower lip, pushing for admittance. Alex submitted, and their tongues gently massaged each other, with Nick greedily swallowing Alex's passionate moans.

Nick continued to kiss Alex, riding high knowing that the gorgeous boy with the beautiful eyes was letting him physically express his deep desire, and responding so sweetly with the delightful little noises he made.

This is perfect. Alex is perfect. I can't believe I'm kissing him.

Chapter 7

ALEX WAS in a state of shock. This handsome, sweet, caring man was kissing him! And at his front door, no less! His big strong arms were wound tightly around him, holding him firmly. The heat of his muscular body was both comforting and deeply arousing.

I can't believe he's kissing me!

Alex had only been kissed once before, but it was nothing like this. Jack had kissed him forcefully after their first date, but there was no passion in his kiss. Nick was making his whole body feel like it was on fire. It was amazing, and a little overwhelming. Alex couldn't think straight. His senses were overloading, as if every nerve in his body was firing at once.

Nick broke the kiss when their mutual need for oxygen forced the issue. Alex's head was swimming. A pleasant lightheadedness that befuddled his usually sharp and wary mind.

"So, are you going to invite me if for coffee?" Nick asked smoothly as he pressed gentle kisses up Alex's neck, occasionally stopping to bite then lick at that sensitive pulse point that made Alex's eyes roll into the back of his head.

"Are you planning on throwing it at me?" Alex replied without thinking, "Oh my God! I'm so sorry. I can't believe I just said that! You've got me so scattered." Alex pulled away and opened the front door, motioning for Nick to enter.

"No worries, it's good to know I found a hot spot, guaranteed to make you lose your mind." Nick smiled wolfishly, heading inside making himself comfortable on the couch. As Alex locked the front door behind him and punched in the code for the alarm system, it suddenly occurred to him what he had just done. He'd invited someone into his house. A visitor. Alex didn't have visitors – ever. Nick had him so rattled, he didn't even notice he had broken his own rules until it was too late.

This man is dangerous. He's making me let my guard down.

Alex would make him some coffee, then try to get him to leave. He dashed into the kitchen, grabbed a couple of mugs from the cupboard and began wrangling the coffee machine of death. Despite his successes earlier that afternoon, the machine was now refusing to work. Alex swore under his breath and kept trying to get the loathsome machine to cooperate.

"Having problems?" Nick said smoothly in Alex's ear, wrapping his arms around his waist, kissing that spot on his neck again.

"If you want coffee, you better stop distracting me." Alex said absently, not really caring if the coffee ever got made. He wouldn't need any so long as Nick kept working that spot on his neck.

Nick smiled against his throat, gently kissing him there one last time before stepping back, "I know you said you were full from dinner, but I thought you might like to split one of the brownies I brought you. They're to die for when they're fresh, and I want to see what you think of them."

Alex went to the fridge, pulled out the bakery box, and dutifully plated up one of the naughty looking treats. The dark, fudgy brownie was wonderfully moist with a thick layer of frosting. When he turned to tackle the coffee machine again, Alex was shocked to see Nick operating the machine like a pro. Without so much of a hint of frustration, Nick had the troublesome device purring like a kitten as it dispensed the glorious dark liquid.

"How? How did you do that?" Alex spluttered in total disbelief.

"I have the same machine at home. It's a real bitch at first, but once you get the hang of it, it's a dream to use." Nick smiled, with just a hint of cockiness. Ordinarily, Alex would find this kind of arrogance a real turn off, but Nick's self-assuredness wasn't mean spirited or malicious. It was actually kind of hot. Alex wasn't sure how he felt about that, but grabbed the plate and followed Nick into the living room, setting down the brownie on the coffee table as Nick passed him a mug.

They sat on the couch, sipping their coffee in strangely comfortable silence. Nick leant forward and broke off a small piece of the brownie, and held it up to Alex's lips. Alex felt his face get hot.

Why should I be embarrassed by this? The man was just sucking on my neck a few minutes ago!

He opened his mouth and allowed Nick to push the sweet treat into his mouth, his fingertips tracing along his lower lip. Alex closed his eyes and moaned as the sweetness exploded on his tastebuds. The flavour was extraordinary – easily the best brownie he'd ever tasted.

"Hazelnut extract!" Alex blurted out, "They used hazelnut extract in the frosting. It's amazing! I can see why this bakery is you're favourite."

Nick smiled wide, clearly very pleased with himself. He reached over and helped himself to a bite of brownie, "I don't usually treat myself like this, but occasionally it's good to indulge." he said, that wolfish grin back on his face. Something made Alex think that he wasn't talking about the brownie anymore.

Alex could feel himself blushing again, but before he could say anything, Nick pressed their lips together again, his arms wrapping around him and guiding Alex to lay back on the couch, Nick sliding on top of him.

Alex could see stars behind his closed eyes, the heady feeling of being held and kissed by such a warm, powerful man being the most erotic thing he had ever experienced. He whimpered as Nick gently nibbled on his lower lip, tugging gently and growling appreciatively, the shared taste of chocolate and hazelnut on their tongues.

Nick slid his hands down Alex's sides gently then up to his chest, the motion startling Alex, making his body stiff and tense, "Stop, please stop." Alex said breathlessly, scrambling to sit up. Nick stopped immediately and pulled away.

"Are you okay? Did I hurt you?" concern clear in his eyes.

"I'm sorry. I'm sorry. I panicked. I'm... I'm not used to being touched like that. I haven't..." Alex cut himself off, not wanting to discuss this, suddenly embarrassed at his outburst. He looked away, so Nick wouldn't see his shame.

"Hey, look at me. You never have to apologise for being upset or scared. I'm sorry if I did anything to upset you. Do you want to talk about it?" Nick gently held Alex's hand and used his thumb to make soothing circles on his skin.

"No, it's just... I can't talk about it. Look, it's getting late, and I'm tired. And I have an early start tomorrow. Maybe we should call it a night?" Alex knew he was babbling, but he was still a little panicked.

"Okay, but just so you know, we can take this as slow as you like. I don't want to push you into doing anything you aren't ready for. I'm happy just hanging out with you if that makes you more comfortable."

Alex started to calm down, the sincerity of his words acting as a balm on his wounded soul. He wasn't pushing. He wasn't forcing. He wasn't angry Alex had asked him to stop. Maybe he didn't need to be afraid of Nick.

"So, would you like to go out to dinner with me again?" Nick said gently, his eyes hopeful. Alex knew going out in public was dangerous, but couldn't think of a reasonable excuse for refusing.

"How about something different?" Nick suggested, "How about you come around to my house sometime. We could do a movie night – order a pizza, watch some trashy movies and just hang out. It'll be fun. No pressure, I promise."

Alex liked the idea of that. It would count as going out, but not in public. He had to admit, the idea of spending more time with Nick was appealing. And a movie night seemed like fun.

"Okay, that sounds great. When do you want to do it?"

"Well, how about tomorrow night? I could pick you up after work?" excitement clear in Nick's eyes. Alex wasn't sure about this. He should drive there himself, so he has the option to leave if he needs to. Not that he expected trouble, but given how many rules he was breaking already, and he was enjoying throwing caution to the wind for the first time in years, he still needed to be sensible.

"No, I'll drive myself. Save you the extra driving. We should exchange numbers. My new phone should arrive tomorrow. You can text me your address." Nick pulled his phone out of his pocket and added Alex's number to his contacts. He quickly texted his address to Alex's number.

"There, done. When you set up your new phone, you'll have a text waiting for you," Nick smiled warmly, "Movie Night starts at 7pm sharp!"

"I look forward to it. Thank you for inviting me."

Nick gave him a gentle, chaste kiss, "No, thank you. You have no idea how happy I am that I get to spend more time with you. And thank you for a delightful evening. I'll see you tomorrow night."

Nick stood, grabbed his keys off the coffee table and made his way to the front door. He stopped when he saw the garbage bag and ruined messenger bag by the door.

"Want me to drop these in the bin on the way out?"

"Oh, yes, I completely forgot about them earlier. Thanks!" Alex beamed, unlocking the door as Nick grabbed the garbage and stepped out.

He turned back to Alex as he stepped onto the porch and smiled, "I can't wait to see you again." and deposited the bags in the big outside bin before heading out to his car and driving away.

Alex locked the front door and activated the security system, then washed up the plate and coffee mugs. Moving into the bathroom, he stripped off his clothes. As he changed into his sleepwear, he saw himself in the big mirror and cringed. Alex could barely stand to look at himself. He couldn't understand why Nick seemed to like him so much.

Because he hasn't seen the real me.

Alex pulled on an old t shirt and got comfortable in bed. He knew this thing with Nick was temporary. It could never last. Better not get used to all this affection, despite Nick saying how much he likes Alex.

He won't want me anymore once he realises I'm damaged goods.

Alex pushed the thought out of his mind and snuggled down under the covers. He forced himself to relax and soon slipped into a dreamless sleep.

The next morning, Alex had a quick breakfast, cleaned up the kitchen then set up for filming. Today he would be making some Red Velvet Cupcakes. Once the camera was set up, the lighting rig on and all the ingredients measured and ready to use, Alex began filming the video, starting with making the batter.

At around eleven o'clock, the cupcakes were baked and cooling on a wire rack. Once they were completely cooled, he would continue filming the video and finish decorating the freshly baked treats. He decided to take the opportunity to make some coffee and have a well deserved rest. His shoulder was still hurting from yesterday's collision, but the muscles surrounding it were starting to calm down. As the coffee started brewing, the machine cooperating for once, there was a sharp knock on the front door, followed by the sound of a car driving away.

Alex walked over to the security monitor by the front door to take a look outside. He'd forgotten to close and lock the iron door last night. Again. He needed to be more careful. Looking at the feed from the porch camera, he could see a box sitting near the front door.

Must have been the courier. My new phone is here!

Alex unlocked the front door and stepped outside, but stopped short when he saw the box was far too big to be his new phone. The box was long, with a small card stuck on the lid. Bending down and removing the lid, Alex saw it was a dozen long stem red roses. Beautiful. He picked up the box and brought it inside. The flowers had an extraordinary scent. He set them down on the kitchen table, intending to put them in a vase once he was finished with filming. He removed the card from the envelope and smiled at the message:

'I can't wait to see you again'

Nick. How unbelievably kind. What a romantic thing to do. The roses are absolutely gorgeous, and suddenly, Alex had an idea. He was going to Nick's house tonight, and his Mum had always said that you should never show up to someone's house empty handed. He looked to the cooling cupcakes on the wire rack. He still needed to decorate them, but Nick's unexpected gift had sparked Alex's imagination. He immediately went through his cake decorating cupboard. He would need a few things to put his plan into action.

Chapter 8

NICK COULD barely contain his excitement. It was Friday, the end of his working week, but more importantly it was Movie Night with Alex in just a few hours. At around lunchtime, he texted Alex to make sure he didn't want Nick to pick him up after work. Clearly his new phone had been delivered on time, because Alex replied shortly afterwards that he would be more comfortable driving himself.

Nick understood his concerns. Alex was clearly uncomfortable with the idea of going to a virtual stranger's home, or possibly just leaving his own home in general. He wondered why Alex seemed to be living in such self-imposed isolation. Did he have some kind of social anxiety? Was he afraid of leaving his house? Was there a specific reason for this? Nick wanted to ask, but realised that Alex wasn't comfortable opening up to him yet. Hopefully after tonight, they would have had a chance to get to know each other better, and Alex would be willing to lower his barriers a little.

Alex sent a second text a few minutes later saying that he would be bringing a little gift to repay his kindness. Nick wasn't sure what that meant exactly, but he was just happy that Alex was still coming, and not texting to cancel which, given Alex's apparent skittishness, was something Nick had suspected may happen.

Nick really liked Alex. It was more than just a physical thing, but Nick couldn't quite put his finger on what it was about Alex that called to him on such a deep, emotional level. Maybe it was because Alex seemed to be a study in contradictions. He was both vulnerable and fiery. So shy, yet so forthright. Alex was also very mysterious. He rarely talked about himself or his past, leaving Nick desperate to find out more. But Nick had always loved a good puzzle.

Nick hoped tonight wasn't too much for Alex. He really did want to get to know him better, but didn't want to push Alex into anything he wasn't comfortable with. Last night on the couch, Alex had seemed to be very much into their little make out session, but then, as if a switch had been flipped inside his head, Alex had suddenly panicked.

Did he have some kind of intimacy issue? Perhaps he is simply inexperienced?

Nick really hoped he could convince Alex to spend the night, or maybe the whole weekend with him, but only if Alex wanted to. He would never force Alex to do anything that would make him uncomfortable.

Nick's work day was dragging on endlessly. Today's agenda had consisted of a few meetings, some paperwork and a quick trip out to the company's new CBD gym to inspect the recently installed remedial massage suites. Keeping busy usually made the work day go faster, but today it seemed to be slowing time to a standstill. Nick was now complete preoccupied with the coming evening, and any attempt to concentrate on the various documents and emails he needed to review was quickly becoming pointless. Eventually, he powered down his laptop, slipped it into his briefcase and told Andrew to bring the car around. It was five o'clock, and he was done for the week.

Traffic was pretty smooth for the most part as Andrew drove them toward Nick's house. The rain, which had been battering the city almost non stop for four days, had finally blown out to sea and the afternoon was mild and sunny, the sky a gorgeous arrangement of blue and streaked white.

When they pulled up at his house, Nick thanked Andrew for all his hard work that week and told him to enjoy his weekend.

"Oh, I will. I'll return the car to the office, then my weekend can finally begin! You have a good weekend too, boss." Andrew said with a grin. Nick returned his smile.

"Well, I'll certainly try, and don't do anything I wouldn't do!" he said with a chuckle as Andrew pulled away. He walked up the driveway and unlocked the front door.

Nick had bought his house a few years ago and had it completely remodelled. The original house, while not falling apart, was certainly in desperate need of some TLC. It hadn't been renovated in decades and the exterior especially was in a terrible state. But despite all these draw backs, the house had good bones and was in an up-and-coming suburb in easy driving distance to the CBD. So Nick got his architect friend to take a look at the house, and he designed something that would not only tidy the place up, but suit his busy lifestyle. The result was a gorgeous, modern tri-level home. 6 double-sized bedrooms upstairs; a spacious open plan living room downstairs; a combined kitchen and dining area with walk-in pantry and all the modern kitchen appliances; a brand new covered entertaining deck overlooking the pool in the back yard; and, Nick's favourite, the basement level had been converted into a huge media room and private gym. Nick loved his home, but had to admit he mostly stuck to his bedroom and the media room. He rarely spent time at home, and when he did, Nick just wanted to relax and hang out, with maybe a bit of cooking on the weekend when he felt like it.

Nick noticed the house had been thoroughly cleaned from top to bottom. His ever efficient housekeeper, Mrs Jenkins, usually came around twice a week to keep the place tidy. But she had made an extra trip today to make sure everything was perfect after he had called and told her he was having a special guest visiting this weekend. When Nick got to the kitchen, he saw several bags on the kitchen table containing the items he had asked Mrs Jenkins to pick up at the supermarket. One bag contained a selection of snacks, including chips, crackers and a selection of dips, which were in a seperate cooler bag. The other bag contained various drinks.

Nick gathered up the bags and headed downstairs to the media room. He switched on the soft lighting and set to work arranging the snacks on the wide coffee table. He placed the drinks and dips in the glass-fronted, full size fridge in the corner, then made certain the big, comfy leather recliners were in the perfect position in front of the big screen. Satisfied everything was as it should be, he returned upstairs, put away the empty shopping bags and looked at the clock on the kitchen wall. Six o'clock. Just enough time to shower, shave, dress and double check his bedroom was presentable, not that he was entirely sure it would be seen by anyone other than himself. But a man could dream. Nick busied himself getting ready. Alex would be here very soon, and he wanted to make a very good impression.

From the shadows of the laneway, he watched as 'Alex' locked the iron door, opened the garage, reversed his car out and drove away. For someone who has been living in hiding for so long, he seemed to have a busy social life.

Alex? No wonder it took so long to find him. And he knew exactly where 'Alex' would be going tonight, and it filled him with a burning, murderous rage.

How could he run away from me? How could he hide for all these years? Doesn't he understand how much I love him? Now, after all that, he cheats on me too? I don't know why I love him so much when he treats me like this.

Trying to keep his temper under control, he turned and walked out of the laneway. He would win 'Alex' back soon. No matter what it took.

Chapter 9

ALTHOUGH ALEX enjoyed driving, he had little call to do it much these days. He didn't initially bother getting himself a car when he first moved to Melbourne, but it quickly became apparent that relying entirely on public transport, even cabs and ride shares, wasn't always the best choice when trying to get in and out of somewhere quickly and with a minimum of exposure. Occasionally, public transport was a necessary evil, especially in the CBD where parking was scarce, but a few months after moving in to his little house, Alex had caved in and purchased a tidy little SUV with tinted windows and all the modern bells and whistles.

Once Alex was satisfied the house was secure, he jumped in his car, which he kept in the small lock up garage next to his house, punched in Nick's address into the GPS system on the dashboard and headed out into the evening traffic. The rain had finally gone and while the traffic was heavy in places, he had a smooth run to the up-scale neighbourhood that Nick apparently called home. Row after row of beautiful houses, immaculate gardens and driveways populated by expensive luxury cars made it clear that Alex had entered a world that he himself could easily live in, if he were interested in splashing his wealth around and making a spectacle of himself. But that was the last thing he could ever do. Alex did not want to draw undue attention. Not if he wanted to stay alive.

It was at that thought he began to wonder if his choice to come over to Nick's house was a wise decision. Leaving the house for any reason was a serious risk to his security and safety, but doing so for such a frivolous reason seemed irrational at best, and downright foolish at worst. But he'd been living in hiding for so many years, trapped in a lonely existence without friends, family or the simple comfort of having other people in his life. The lure of the handsome, kind and generous man who seemed to be keen to get to know someone like Alex, despite his obvious faults and failings, was damn near irresistible. But Alex was aware that just because someone appeared to be interested in him, didn't mean they were telling the truth. It didn't mean their intentions were pure or that they were indeed as harmless as they appeared.

But Alex looked around at the neighbourhood as he pulled up to the address the GPS indicated and felt like this was a safe place. There was nobody walking down the street. The whole area was neat, clean and friendly. The road was well lit with plenty of streetlights to chase away the evening shadows. He looked toward what was apparently Nick's home and stifled a gasp. It was huge. Less of a house, more of a mansion. Okay, probably not a mansion per se, but Nick's home was certainly far from the average Australian home. The front yard was neatly landscaped and featured a variety of native Australian plants, with a large marble bird bath in the centre of an expansive, perfectly manicured lawn. The brick driveway was clean and free of fallen leaves from the imposing Jacaranda tree that covered half of the house from view. The house itself was modern, with grey rendered walls, black roof tiles and large picture windows.

Alex got out of the car, grabbed his cane and the spare backpack he had found tucked away in his bedroom wardrobe, and slowly made his way up the driveway toward the oversized stained wood front door. He grasped the ornate brass knocker and gave it a few sharp knocks, then waited. Moments later, the large door opened, and there stood Nick. Alex's mouth went dry and he lost the ability to form words. Nick was wearing a pair of faded blue jeans, a super tight black t shirt that accentuated every muscle in his enormous torso. He was also barefoot. A total departure from the GQ type wardrobe that Alex had quickly become accustomed to seeing Nick wear. Alex hadn't been sure what he should wear tonight, but since Nick had said it was 'casual' and he had liked Alex's clothing choices last night, he had elected to go with a similar outfit. Plain chinos, a red polo shirt and his comfortable yet clean sneakers.

"Alex! I'm so glad you could make it. Please come on in." Nick said smoothly as his sharp gaze swept over Alex's form, his face relaxed with a satisfied grin. He stepped aside and allowed Alex to come in, offering to take his bag and closing the door behind him. Alex quickly removed his shoes and socks, then placed them on the wooden shoe rack by the door. The large, open living room was cool, modern but seemed very impersonal. The only furniture was a glass and metal coffee table and a large black leather couch with matching arm chairs. A stark modern art canvas on the wall opposite the couch was the only ornamentation, There was no television that he could see, which didn't seem to make sense given they were supposed to be having a movie night. Maybe the TV was in another room? Alex suspected this room had been decorated by someone else, probably some expensive interior designer, and Nick likely spent little time in here.

"Your home is beautiful. Thanks for inviting me. Um, nice couch." he struggled to say, hoping his compliment didn't sound disingenuous, but he didn't want to insult his host by saying his living room looked barren and sterile.

"Thanks. The couch is fairly comfy, but I rarely sit on it. Not when I have everything I need downstairs. Come on, I'll show you my man cave." Nick said with a devilish grin as he placed his hand on Alex's lower back and gently escorted him toward a carpeted staircase near the entry to what looked like a spacious kitchen. They descended into a large, softly lit downstairs room that must be the basement.

Alex must have looked slightly apprehensive, because Nick leaned in from behind and said "Trust me, Alex. You're going to love it." his warm breath making Alex shiver with arousal.

How does he make me feel like this, just with his voice alone?

At the bottom of the stairs, Alex stepped into an enormous room that could only be described as a movie lover's dream. The rear of the room was dominated by a giant cinema sized TV screen, virtually the same size as the screens at the little independent movie house in

Alex's home town. The screen even had large red drapes on either side, giving the room a very theatrical look. Below the screen was a low cabinet containing all sorts of cutting edge media equipment, such as a Blu-ray player, an Apple TV, a sound bar, stereo system, games consoles and more. On the right wall was several built in cabinets featuring a dizzying array of DVDs, Blu-rays, old VHS video tapes and music on both CD and vinyl. The opposite wall featured a large, well stocked drinks fridge, some book cases featuring hundreds of books; and a small work desk with a laptop and a desk lamp. The centre of the room featured two huge leather recliners, each with electronic controls and drink holders. A big wooden coffee table, which sat between the chairs and the screen, was covered in snacks, dips, paper napkins and eating utensils. Alex was speechless. This was an amazing room, and he could see himself getting lost in here for hours exploring the books and movies.

"So, what do you think? This is my favourite room in the house. My little sanctuary from the outside world." Nick was clearly proud of his 'man cave' and he had every right to be. It was an impressive sight, and must have cost a fortune to put together.

"It's amazing!" Alex said, "I've heard of people having their own home cinemas, but this is something else. Guess you're a bit of a couch potato, eh?" he chuckled teasingly.

"Well, I do like to relax, but I try to balance things out." Nick said smiling, walking toward a closed door next to the stairs. Opening it revealed a large home gym featuring a wide array of exercise equipment, most of which Alex couldn't identify if you paid him.

"I guess the owner of a chain of gyms would need to have his own gym at home. Wouldn't be good for the business if you lost you're physique." Alex said.

Nick smiled wolfishly and slowly ran his hand up and down his rippling stomach muscles, "So, you noticed my physique, did you?" his voice low and sexy.

Alex's mouth went dry again as he watched his host's hand in it's hypnotic movement over the tight t shirt, but managed to choke out "Difficult to miss in that outfit." which made Nick smile even wider.

"Why don't we take a look at my movie collection and decide what we want to watch. Then I'll order dinner and we can begin our night of couch potatoing."

Nick waved his arm towards the large cabinets on the right. Alex was surprised at the wide selection of movies in Nick's collection. A variety of genres, including all the latest blockbusters, some world cinema classics and a huge selection of old school movies.

"How about a good old fashioned horror movie?" Nick suggested, "Nothing like a slasher on Movie Night." he said with a warm smile, holding up the DVD case for 'Halloween' - a suggestion that must have made Alex visibly shudder, because Nick's smile instantly fell.

"Are you okay?" he asked, his eyes etched with concern, "Not a fan of horror movies?"

My life is a horror movie.

"Not really, I find them a little too..." but couldn't finish his sentence. The memories of that night came flooding back, and Alex desperately tried to cram them down and maintain his composure.

"No worries, we can watch something else. What kind of movies *do* you like?" Nick replaced the offending DVD back on the shelf and moved along to the next cabinet.

Alex calmed himself and moved along to see the rest of the movies, "I like old school Sci Fi flicks. 'Forbidden Planet' is excellent, as is 'The Day The Earth Stood Still' - the original, not the garbage Keanu Reeves remake, which was an insult to classic movie lovers everywhere!" Alex enjoyed cheesy old B movies, and judging by some of the title's in the middle cabinet, Nick clearly was too. Who would have thought they had such similar tastes?

"How about 'Plan 9 From Outer Space' for a bit of cheesy science fiction goodness?" Nick said, holding up a DVD case, almost as if he had read Alex's mind.

"Oh my God! I love Plan 9! It's the worst movie ever made! And it's absolutely perfect. Ed Wood was a demented genius," Alex gushed. He couldn't believe this giant, muscle-bound man loved these types of movies. Apparently that old saying 'never judge a book by it's cover' continued to be true.

With that, Nick grabbed 'Forbidden Planet' and the original version of 'The Day The Earth Stood Still' off the shelf too, took all three movies over to the Blu-ray player, and loaded them into the multi-disc carousel.

"Now that the evening's entertainment has been decided upon, let's order our pizzas and get settled in." Nick said as he lowered himself into one of the comfy-looking leather recliners and beckoned Alex to join him. All this talk of food had suddenly reminded him of the gift he had brought for Nick. He opened the back pack, which Nick had placed next to the vacant recliner, pulled out a sturdy plastic food storage box, then handed it to his host.

"This is my contribution to the evening's festivities, and a little thank you for your kindness and generosity. You inspired me today." he said as he handed the box to Nick.

"You didn't have to bring me anything. But thank you very much, Alex. May I open it now?" Nick said with a gleeful grin on his face. In that moment, he looked like a little boy on Christmas morning, and Alex's heart swelled at the knowledge that he was responsible for that beaming smile. Alex nodded and watched as Nick carefully pulled the plastic lid off the box, revealing half a dozen Red Velvet Cupcakes, each lovingly decorated with beautiful edible roses, just like the one's Nick had sent today.

"Wow, these are amazing. The detail is exquisite. The flowers almost look real. You must have spent hours making these. Thank you so much." Nick looked genuinely pleased by his gift, awe-struck even, and he suddenly launched himself out of the recliner, placed the box on the coffee table, and enveloped Alex in a powerful embrace, kissing him deeply. Alex was lost in the moment, feeling himself crushed against the man's hard muscles, every inch of him seared by Nick's body heat. He felt floaty and warm, and moaned as Nick deepened the kiss. When he broke the kiss and allowed them both to suck in some precious oxygen, Nick placed his hands on either side of Alex's head, staring deeply into his eyes.

"I've never received such a beautiful gift before. Thank you."

Alex was unable to form words, so he just nodded his flushed face and smiled. He still felt a little giddy. This man could melt through every one of his defences, and in this moment in time, Alex didn't have a care in the world. He lowered himself into the large leather recliner and used the buttons on the armrest to adjust it's position to a comfortable configuration. Once he found the sweet spot, he let out an unconscious growl of approval.

"You think that's comfy, try this." Nick said, pressing one of the button's on Alex's armrest. The chair started to gently vibrate, sending tingling sensations up his spine and carefully relaxing every muscle in his back, melting away his tension.

"Oh my God, that's... my spine feels like it's liquifying! If it wasn't an affront to God, I think I might actually marry this chair!" Alex joked as his eyes slipped closed and focused on the glorious massage function.

"Wow, I didn't think I'd be in competition with a piece of furniture, but I guess I can't really blame you. These chairs are pretty awesome," Nick chuckled, "Should I put these cupcakes in the fridge?"

Alex opened his eyes reluctantly and focussed on Nick, "No, they'll be fine on the table, unless you expect a heatwave in the next couple of hours," he said, turning off the massage function. If he left it on much longer, he'd be a giant pile of goo.

"Well, there might just be some heat later, but I don't think it'll be the cupcakes in danger of melting." Nick grinned, waggling his eyebrows suggestively.

"You need to work on your pick up lines. That one was atrocious!" Alex groaned and giggled, "Although at least you've stopped throwing drinks at me." he added, smirking.

Nick burst out laughing, "You're never going to let that go are you?" trying to look offended, but his laughter betraying his obvious amusement.

"Okay, I promise not to mention it again," Alex said, trying to look serious and solemn, "Unless it's still funny. In that case, I'll just keep squeezing every last drop out of it!" Alex enjoyed the teasing back and forth between them. Nick was clearly not offended by the teasing, as he was laughing too.

"Alright, smartypants, enough with the coffee jokes. What would you like on your pizza?" Nick asked, picking up his phone from the coffee table in front of them and opened a food delivery app, "I like a good Meatlovers pizza with lots of barbecue sauce." he suggested, which Alex thought sounded good.

"I haven't had pizza since I was a little kid. Do they still make the one with ham and pineapple?" Alex queried.

Nick looked momentarily confused, but smiled and said "Hawaiian? Sure they do. One Hawaiian and one Meatlovers coming right up. Oh, and garlic bread, because you gotta have garlic bread with pizza." Nick busied himself putting the order into his phone.

"Why don't you grab us a couple of drinks from the fridge while I set up the first movie?" Nick asked as he switched to a remote control app and started turning on all the media equipment. Alex stood up and went over to the drinks fridge in the corner, marvelling at the variety of options.

"What would you like?" Alex enquired, grabbing himself a can of Mountain Dew.

"I'll have a beer, thanks" Nick said, and Alex grabbed a bottle of Bondi Blonde.

He returned to his seat and handed the bottle to Nick, who smiled his appreciation and twisted off the bottle cap, taking a long pull of the beer. Alex watched Nick's Adam's apple bob up and down as he swallowed, and he felt his pulse quicken at the sight. Why did he find that so alluring? Alex tried to concentrate on his own drink, the flavour sweet and tangy.

"Can I ask you a personal question?" Nick said, his tone soft. Alex tensed slightly, but nodded his agreement.

"Before yesterday, when was the last time you left your house? I mean, actually left the house and went out somewhere, not just to put the bins out or something?"

Alex hadn't expected that question. He wasn't really sure how to answer. He cast his mind back to his last expedition to the outside world. *When had that been? It can't have been too long ago, surely?*

"Um, I had to go out to renew my driver's licence, that was a couple of months before Christmas, I think?" Alex said hesitantly.

"So, about eight months? And before that?" Nick's face looked concerned for some reason. Was eight months really so unusual? It had been so long since he had regular interactions with other people, he wasn't really sure anymore.

"I don't know. I told you I don't get out much these days." Alex didn't want to talk about this, but he also didn't want to be rude to Nick.

"Is there a reason you don't you go out more often?"

"Yes, but I don't want to talk about it," Alex looked desperately around the room for a distraction, "So, how about we get this Movie Night started? I'm ready when you are!" he said with hopefully enough enthusiasm that Nick would just start the movie and not continue to delve into Alex's past. Nick seemed to accept Alex's reluctance to continue this conversation and he tapped an icon on his phone's screen.

The lights in the room slowly dimmed and then winked out. The giant screen came on, and with a couple of taps, Nick had the first movie loading up. Moments later, 'The Day The Earth Stood Still' appeared on screen in gloriously remastered black and white. The only light in the room now came from the huge cinema screen, as Klaatu's flying saucer descended from the sky. Alex's hand sat on the armrest, and Nick reached over and placed his hand over it, squeezing it reassuringly, only releasing it when Nick's phone indicated that dinner had arrived. Alex offered to go get the food, but Nick told him to relax and enjoy the movie, and with that he dashed up the stairs to meet the delivery driver. When he returned with the pizzas and garlic bread, the two men enjoyed their meal, swapping slices and quoting the famous lines from the movie.

Alex felt relaxed and safe, and couldn't remember having this much fun watching a movie. Nick had seen this film almost as many times as he had, and his scathingly sarcastic commentary about the dodgy special effects had Alex crying with laughter.

When the film finished, Nick turned the lights back on and grabbed the box containing the cupcakes.

"Dessert time! I've been looking forward to these." he said with that same boyish grin from earlier. He opened the box and pulled out two of the cupcakes, passing one to Alex.

"I hope you enjoy them. They're Red Velvet with vanilla bean cream cheese frosting, and the roses are made with hand painted modelling chocolate..." Alex was cut off at the sight of Nick sensuously licking a small amount of the frosting off his cupcake, his long tongue flicking across his lips as he moaned his appreciation. Alex blushed and felt himself getting hard. Nick's fiery gaze focussed in on Alex, searing him to the spot.

"Absolutely delicious," Nick said smoothly, "This frosting is amazing. Here, try some," he said, scooping up a dollop of the sweet frosting with his finger and holding it up to Alex's lips. Alex tried to say he already knew what it tasted like, after all – he made it, but as soon as he parted his lips, Nick pushed his finger gently into his open mouth. Alex closed his lips instinctively around the intruding digit, sucking the treat into his mouth. His tastebuds were awakened by the combination of sweetness from the frosting and saltiness from Nick's skin. He closed his eyes and let out a whimper. Nick growled with pleasure as he reluctantly pulled his finger out of Alex's warm wet mouth.

If Alex blushed any more, his face would probably catch fire. He'd never felt like this before. So turned on. So wanton. Nick smiled at Alex's obvious arousal, simply saying "So sweet."

"Yeah," Alex said, trying to focus on words, "I used icing sugar."

Nick smiled wolfishly, "I wasn't talking about the frosting." and turned the lights off again as the next movie began. Once they finished eating their cupcakes, Nick returned to holding Alex's hand, running his thumb in soothing circles on the back of his hand.

Once they had watched the two remaining films, and laughed themselves senseless at the epic awfulness that is 'Plan 9 From Outer Space' Nick switched on the lights and powered down the media equipment. He stood and bent down in front of Alex, his big hands covering Alex's smaller hands.

"You are so beautiful." Nick said breathlessly, staring deep into his eyes.

"I'm really not." Alex said dismissively, lowering his eyes. Nick placed a finger under his chin and raised his head to meet his gaze

"Hey. Don't ever put yourself down. You. Are. Beautiful." and with that, he pressed their lips together, interlacing their fingers.

"Spend the night with me. Please Alex, don't go home."

Alex wasn't sure about this. It was late, he should go home, and as he started to mumble his uncertainties, Nick started to kiss up the side of Alex's neck, sucking, biting and licking in that spot that made Alex lose his senses. His resistance was quickly crumbling and he couldn't contain his soft whimpers and moans as Nick's ministrations left him breathless and panting.

"Please, Alex. You don't have to do anything you're not comfortable with. You can spend the night with me, or you can stay in one of the guest rooms."

Alex was unable to resist this man any longer. His libido was out of control and his body felt like it was on fire.

"I think... I think I'd like to spend the night with you." Alex said, watching as Nick's expression went from hopeful to overjoyed.

Nick kissed him again, this time holding his head with both hands, taking control of the kiss, pressing him back in the recliner. When Nick broke the kiss and eased him out of the chair, Alex was smiling and flushed. He allowed Nick to gently escort him up the stairs, all the way to the top floor of the house, and toward the master bedroom.

Chapter 10

NICK ALMOST felt like pinching himself. Alex had actually agreed to spend the night with him. He was giddy with excitement, but he kept his emotions in check. It was clear that Alex was still very nervous, and the last thing Nick wanted to do was to make him feel pressured in any way. Nick was also a little stunned by Alex's earlier revelation that he hadn't left his own home for over eight months. This went a long way to explaining Alex's rusty social skills, but an explanation for *why* he isolated himself in such a manner was not yet forthcoming. Regardless of the reason, Nick was willing to go as slow as Alex wanted and he would happily take things one step at a time.

When they reached the landing of the top floor, he pulled Alex into a warm embrace and nuzzled into his boy's sweet neck. He lay down featherlight kisses across Alex's skin, then pressed their lips together, slow and gentle.

"Like I said earlier, you don't have to do anything you don't want to do. You can sleep with me in my bed or, if you prefer, you can sleep in one of the guest rooms. Whatever you want to do, I promise is fine with me."

Alex looked deep into his eyes, indecision clear on his face. How long had it been since Alex had been with another man? Had he ever been with another man? Even the simplest touches seemed surprising, even alien to him. Nick suspected if Alex wasn't a virgin, it had been a considerable amount of time since he was last intimate with someone. All the more reason to take things slow.

"I think..." Alex said softly, almost shyly, "I think I'd like to sleep in your bed, if that's okay. I mean, if you'd rather me sleep in the guest..." Nick cut him off with a ravaging kiss. His boy wanted to sleep with him. Nick was overjoyed. Again, he had to remind himself not to be too excited. One step at a time.

A long, slow seduction. Respect Alex's limits. Make him comfortable. Don't push.

"That's more than okay," Nick said breathlessly when he broke the kiss, "Come with me and I'll show you my room," and with that, he lead Alex by the hand down the hall, toward the back of the house. They entered the large master bedroom and Nick walked over and switched on one of the bedside lamps. The room filled with soft light revealing a spacious chamber that was warm, masculine and very much decorated to suit Nick's tastes. It was dominated by a wooden, king size four poster bed with matching side tables in the centre of the room. To the left was a walk-in wardrobe with dressing room and a beautifully appointed ensuite with a double sized shower. On the other side of the room, a pair of gorgeous French doors led out to the wide balcony overlooking the backyard and pool area. The view of the night sky and the shining full moon was breathtakingly beautiful.

"If you'd like to freshen up, the bathroom is just through there." Nick said, pointing toward the ensuite. Alex nodded nervously, then slowly withdrew to the bathroom, closing the door behind him. Nick pulled back the covers on the neatly made bed, then set about removing his jeans. He consciously decided not to strip off any other clothes at this time as he didn't want to be presumptuous, or worse, intimidating. Dressed only in his t shirt and soft black boxer briefs, he stretched out on the bed and waited for Alex to emerge.

The click of the bathroom door drew Nick's attention. Alex stepped out. He had removed his jeans, and was clutching them protectively over his boxer shorts. He slowly limped over to the bed, dropped the jeans on the floor and set his cane against the bedside table. He climbed onto the bed and settled next to Nick. Alex looked very nervous. He was almost shaking. Nick needed to reassure him.

"Hey, remember, you don't have to do anything you don't want to do. We can go straight to sleep, or we can do some more kissing and stuff. No pressure. No expectations. We go at your pace."

Alex seemed to relax a little, Nick watching the tension melt away from his shoulders. That beautiful shy blush stained his cheeks, and Nick took that as Alex's way of showing he'd like to do something other than sleep. Alex was very submissive, and Nick loved that about him. He reached over, cupping the back of Alex's head, and drew him into a soft kiss. Alex moaned and melted into Nick's embrace. He surrendered himself to the moment and slowly opened his lips, granting Nick access to his warm, willing mouth. Nick glided his tongue along Alex's soft, plump lips, teasing and tasting. He slowly lowered his hands to Alex's shoulders, caressing and massaging the tense muscles, then worked his way down his boy's arms. Alex relaxed, leaning back slightly, his shirt riding up slightly and revealing a thin strip of skin along his lower belly. Nick's fingers traced feather soft touches along the exposed path of skin, but when he attempted to push the shirt up a little more, Alex immediately tensed and grabbed both of Nick's wrists in a surprisingly strong, vice-like grip.

"Stop!" Alex said almost breathlessly. Nick immediately halted his movements.

"I'm sorry. Did I hurt you? I just wanted to take your shirt off." Nick was relieved when Alex released his wrists. His boy was remarkably strong.

"No, I'm sorry. I just..." Alex's eyes were wide with panic, "I don't want to take my shirt off. And trust me, you don't want me to, either." Alex lowered his head and looked very uncomfortable.

Nick had a moment of realisation. Alex was ashamed of his body. He had probably been told by countless guys that being fat was ugly. His boy's self esteem had probably been battered and bruised so much over the years, he probably believed the vile jibes that had been hurled at him.

"Hey, you don't have worry. I don't care that you're chubby. In fact, if you haven't already noticed, I have quite a love for larger guys. I promise, you have nothing to be ashamed of." Nick said with warm sincerity. But Alex didn't seem to relax.

"It's not that. Well, it's not just that. Being fat isn't the main issue. I..." Alex was almost whispering, "I have...scars."

Scars? Had Alex been in an accident? Why would he think I would be put off by that? I need to reassure him.

"I don't care about anything so superficial. I have scars too." he said, and quickly pulled off his own shirt, revealing his bare chest.

Raising his right arm and turning his left side toward Alex, displaying the scar that traced just below his rib cage, "I got this one when I stacked my mountain bike a couple of years ago," then Nick turned his body the opposite direction, showing off a longer scar on his right shoulder blade, "and this one I got falling off my surfboard and smashing against a submerged rock."

Nick hoped that this little 'show and tell' session would be enough to relax Alex and reassure him he had nothing to worry about. But it was clear his boy was still conflicted.

"My scars are bigger, and I have more of them. They're ugly. You... you really don't want to see them." Alex stated, as if he had rehearsed this line in his mind many times. He was genuinely convinced that a few scars would be all it would take to scare away a man like Nick. His heart was breaking at the thought that Alex had convinced himself he was ugly, and all because of something as irrelevant as a few patches of skin. How long had he been carrying this around? Was this why Alex rarely left the house? Nick needed to fix this right now.

"You don't have to take your shirt off if you don't want to, but I promise you, I don't care about any scars. No matter what they look like or how many you have. I like *you,* Alex. You are an amazing, funny, kind, sweet and sexy man. Some scarred skin isn't going to chase me away. I promise, you don't have to worry. You are beautiful. You always will be in my eyes."

Alex appeared to relax a little at Nick's words. He looked up and scanned Nick's face, apparently trying to confirm Nick's sincerity. He took a deep breathe, let it out slowly, then as if he were removing a bandaid, quickly pulled his shirt over his head and clutched it in his lap.

Nick hoped he had adequately schooled his expression, because when he looked over Alex's exposed torso, what he saw shocked him to his core. Nick had been expecting some burns, perhaps a surgical scar or two from a long ago accident. But what he was confronted with was seven jagged scars across his chest and belly. When Alex leaned forward slightly, Nick spotted two more jagged scars either side of his lower spine. These were not the result of cutting himself. He had not been involved in some kind of horrible accident. Nor would any reputable surgeon leave scars like this after any kind of operation.

Alex had apparently been the victim of a frenzied stabbing attack.

Chapter 11

ALEX WAITED for the inevitable look of loathing and disgust on Nick's face. He knew as soon as he took his shirt off, he would shock Nick into speechlessness. Exposing his revolting, damaged form would be the final nail in the coffin, and Nick would at last realise he had been wasting his time pursuing someone like Alex. Although he knew this was how it would always play out, and being rejected was only to be expected, Alex was surprised at how much he would miss Nick when he inevitably worked passed his disgust to politely ask him to get dressed and leave.

Nick's face remained impassive, no look of shock or disgust, but he hadn't said anything yet, and the pregnant pause was getting awkward and uncomfortable. Alex didn't want to draw this out, so he reached for his shirt and went to put it back on, only to be stopped in his tracks by Nick's hands.

"How did you get these scars?" he asked softly, gently, almost as if he wasn't repelled by the gruesome display before him.

Unless he's blind, there's no chance he missed them. Why isn't he reacting? Why isn't he telling me to leave?

"I don't want to talk about it." Alex mumbled, reaching for the shirt again, determined to cover himself up and end this nightmare. But Nick was having none of it. He grabbed the garment from Alex's hands and tossed it to the floor behind him. Alex was totally confused.

Why did he do that? Surely he can't want to look at me.

Nick leaned forward and pressed his lips to Alex's, a soft kiss that felt like magic. That spark of electricity Alex had felt when Nick kissed him earlier was as strong as ever. But why was this happening?

Is he kissing me so he doesn't have to look at my scars? Is he just being nice?

Before Alex could process what was happening, Nick leaned down and lay a gentle kiss on one of Alex's chest scars. He couldn't believe it.

No one had ever done anything like that before. No one had ever been given the chance. Did he really not care about the scars? Was this his way of showing they didn't matter to him? Nick's words from earlier echoed in his mind.

"I like YOU, *Alex."*

Nick was actually being sincere. He genuinely did like him. But surely that was impossible. Had Alex actually met someone who not only liked him, but didn't care about his weight, his rusty social skills or even his damaged body? He was overwhelmed. He almost felt like crying. Never in his wildest dreams did he ever believe that something like this would actually happen to him.

Nick continued kissing his way down Alex's torso, stopping at each of the scars along the way to lovingly kiss and caress them as he passed. He slowly encouraged Alex to lay back and relax as he covered his body with warm, passionate kisses and touches. Nick's expression wasn't of revulsion or pity. His face was filled with awe. He wasn't just loving on Alex, he was worshipping him.

Nick worked his way back up, this time licking his way up to Alex's throat, laving, kissing and nibbling at that spot on his neck that made him go crazy. Alex felt his eyes roll into the back of his head and couldn't contain the moans that were coming from him every time Nick found a hot spot that made his body light up like a Christmas tree.

"You are so beautiful. I'm so lucky to have found you. I'm going to treat you right, I promise. I'm going to make you fly." Nick murmured in his ear, his hot breath stoking the flames that already burned bright within.

"I...um..." Alex tried to find the words, but his mind was flooded with sensations he'd never felt before, "I've never...well...I'm a virgin."

"Don't worry, boy. I'm going to make you feel amazing. Let me take care of you. Let me make you feel good." Nick said as his fingers traced Alex's erection through his boxer shorts. Alex couldn't speak. He just nodded and whimpered as Nick pressed his palm onto Alex's hardness.

Nick calling him 'boy' was the most erotic thing he had ever heard. Alex may be a virgin, but he was no stranger to porn. Seven years alone in his house, porn was pretty much his only sexual outlet. From the various sexy videos he'd watched online, he knew 'boy' was often used in Dom/sub relationships. Alex didn't think much of BDSM. He'd been through enough pain in his life, and the idea of being flogged or whipped for recreational purposes didn't turn him on in the slightest, but Alex had to admit, the idea of being dominated by a larger, alpha male type had always titillated him. Nick didn't look like the type who was into inflicting pain, and nothing he had said or done so far led Alex to believe Nick ever would. But Nick certainly looked like he was in his element, in charge and subtly dominating Alex with his words and his actions. Alex had always fantasised about something like this, but he never thought it would actually happen.

Nick pulled back and carefully slipped off Alex's boxer shorts, tossing them to the floor with the rest of his clothes, then leaned over to the bedside table and got out a bottle of lube. He leaned over Alex again and kissed him long and deep, stopping to suck on his lower lip, which made Alex gasp involuntarily.

"Oh please, Sir." Alex said breathlessly, unconsciously using the honorific, but realising instantly how perfectly it sounded. Nick growled deeply, a wicked grin on his face showing he was pleased with Alex's choice of words. Alex didn't even know what he was asking for exactly. He just didn't want this to stop. Not even the kinkiest porn videos had turned him on this much.

Nick held Alex in place by sliding the fingers of one hand through his hair and gripping gently but firmly. He then moved down the bed slightly and leaned in to nuzzle one of Alex's nipples. He traced the outer edge ever so gently with his tongue, flicking it across the tip from time to time. Alex's response was immediate, moaning with pleasure as his strainingly hard cock began to leak precum. While Nick continued to tease his nipples, giving them little nips with his teeth then soothing them with his tongue, he used his free hand to swipe his thumb across the head of Alex's cock, spreading the sticky fluid along his frenulum, making Alex's balls ache with need.

"I got you boy, I'm going to make you fly." Nick said with a gravelly voice. He reached over for the lube, flipped off the lid and squeezed a small amount onto his hand and spread it over Alex's cock, making it slippery and slick. He took Alex's hardness in his hand and slowly pumped it, making him start to wriggle and shake all over. This was so overwhelming. The sensations were overloading his nerves. Everything felt like a live wire that sparked deep inside. Nick continued to pump slowly, from head to root, steadily increasing the pace as he continued to lick and nibble at Alex's now highly sensitive nipples.

"Oh my God! Oh my God! It's... I can't..." Alex gasped, babbling incoherently. He was only just aware that Nick had at some point removed his own underwear, and Alex could see his thick, erect cock, straining for attention. Alex reached up and grasped it with his left hand and began pumping him too. Nick growled with approval, and moved up slightly to start lavishing attention on Alex's neck and shoulder, licking and biting, nibbling on his earlobe. Alex felt like he was on fire. He continued to pump Nick's huge cock, twisting slightly now and again in that way Alex always enjoyed when he was pleasuring himself.

Nick and Alex were now pumping each other's cocks at a frantic pace, both men breathing hard, almost panting, their respective orgasms quickly building.

"I'm so close." Alex managed to pant out the words, biting his lower lip to stop from screaming.

"Yeah, boy. Shoot it. Give it to me." Nick panted, his lips hovering over the strip of muscle on Alex's shoulder. Alex felt his balls tighten and that tingling sensation at the bottom of his spine. He could no longer contain himself, and let out a cry as Nick bit down on his bare shoulder. Alex shot his load, spraying hot come over his belly and

Nick's hand. Nick roared as he found his own release, coating Alex's hand with sticky white heat.

Both men collapsed on the bed, breathing like there wasn't enough air in the room. As their heart rates dropped back to normal and their breathing levelled out, Nick leaned over and kissed Alex gently.

"That was amazing. You were amazing. Lay there and I'll get something to clean us up." Nick said. He kissed Alex again, then got off the bed and went into the ensuite.

Alex was a pile of boneless goo and couldn't respond if he tried. His mind was shattered. Every nerve in his body felt like it had been burned out. He had never suspected that sex could be anything like that.

Nick returned a few moments later with a warm wash cloth. He lovingly cleaned Alex up and pulled the covers over him. He disposed of the cloth, then joined him in bed, spooning in behind Alex and wrapping him in his arms.

"Sleep now," Nick said, laying a gentle kiss on his back, "I've got you." and together, they fell into a sated, restful sleep.

Chapter 12

NICK WOKE up to the gentle warmth of the early morning sunlight streaming in through the large picture window behind his bed. It was just after eight AM, and he hadn't felt this happy or relaxed in years. Last night had been a rollercoaster of emotions, but he smiled at the knowledge that he had finally managed to break down some of the protective walls that Alex had built around himself. His boy had trusted him enough to not only come around for Movie Night (a massive feat in itself) but had connected with him on several levels, and discovered they had more in common than he could possibly have wished for.

My boy.

Nick couldn't wipe the smile off his face if you paid him. He loved the idea of thinking of Alex as his boy. Alex had been so sweet in bed. He was warm and responsive. His touches had been glorious and unexpected. He'd even called Nick 'Sir' - which confirmed his suspicions that Alex, whether he knew it or not, was a natural submissive. Nick had never really got into the BDSM scene, and didn't really consider himself to be a 'Dom' as such, but he enjoyed being naturally dominant in bed. He wasn't into the whole whips and chains thing, nor did he really like inflicting serious pain. He just liked being in charge, but only ever when he was with someone who enjoyed that. Every day he was discovering more and more about Alex, and each revelation seemed to confirm his gut feelings. For Nick to have found a partner who not only matched his physical ideal, shared many of his interests and seemed to be willing to explore a little domination in the bedroom, it felt like all his Christmases had come at once.

Nick rolled over to cuddle up to his boy, but suddenly realised he was alone in bed. He looked toward the ensuite, but he could see from the open door that Alex wasn't there. Nick noticed that Alex's clothes, which had been strewn around the bedroom floor just a few hours ago, had vanished along with his walking cane.

Had Alex gone home without saying goodbye? Was he upset about something? Did I push him too far too quickly?

Nick's internal worries were interrupted by an enticing aroma that floated into the room through the ajar bedroom door. A rich combination of freshly brewed coffee, something sweet and something spicy. Focusing, he could hear soft noises coming from downstairs. Alex must be in the kitchen, and if Nick's nose was to be believed, his boy was making breakfast.

He jumped out of bed, went into the bathroom and began his morning routine. After quickly showering and brushing his teeth, deciding to skip shaving today, Nick quickly dressed and made his way downstairs to find Alex. As he approached the kitchen, the enticing scents became more pronounced. On the kitchen table was a basket of freshly baked muffins, banana and cinnamon by the smell of them, and a plate of some baked egg things that Nick didn't recognise. What ever they were, they looked and smelled sensational. Looking toward the sink, he found Alex crouched down beside the dishwasher, loading up some dishes.

"Good Morning, Gorgeous," he said softly, startling Alex for a moment, but he instantly relaxed once he turned and saw Nick, "You've certainly been busy. Have you been up all night?"

"Good Morning to you too. I've only been up a couple of hours. I don't usually sleep all the way through the night, and I needed to get up to take my meds anyway. So, I thought I'd come down here and whip up a little something for breakfast. You have a very well stocked kitchen, but I might have gone a little bit overboard. I hope you don't mind," Alex suddenly looked a little hesitant.

"Of course I don't mind," Nick assured him with a smile, "I just can't believe you made all this by yourself. It all looks amazing!"

Alex beamed at the praise, "Don't look so shocked. I don't just make cupcakes you know! I'm pretty well-rounded in the kitchen, but cupcakes pay the bills better."

Nick crossed the room and took Alex into his arms, kissing him deeply and holding him tight, "Thank you for going to all this trouble. I'm very lucky to have found you. You are so special. Now, tell me what we are having for breakfast. I'm starving!" Nick said with a grin.

Alex started the coffee machine and as the coffee mug beneath it began to fill with the hot energising liquid, he explained the items he had prepared.

"I wasn't sure what you normally ate for breakfast, so I decided to do a bit of everything. I made some of my Banana Bread Muffins with cinnamon, nutmeg and allspice; some oven baked mini omelettes with chorizo, spinach and feta cheese; and in the fridge is two bowls of fresh fruit salad with honey, raspberry and mint glaze."

Nick was flabbergasted. This is what Alex called 'whipping up a little something for breakfast?' He'd expect a spread like this in a restaurant, not his own kitchen. His boy was obviously very talented. He watched Alex as he pulled the two serving bowls of fruit salad out of the fridge and place them on the table. They looked less like food, and more like works of art. Alex handed him a steaming mug of coffee, and they both sat down at the table.

"Wow, I can't believe you did all this. You're amazing, Alex. I can't wait to try everything," as he grabbed his fork and began digging into the fruit salad in front of him.

Nick wasn't usually a fan of fruit salad, but he didn't want to hurt Alex's feelings, especially after the considerable effort he had clearly put in to making breakfast, so he dug in heartily. The combination of fruits was delightful, and the thin glaze that Alex had tossed through the salad was sweet, tart and lightly refreshing all at the same time. It was absolutely sublime. Alex may have just changed his attitude toward fruit salad forever. Nick polished off his bowl, practically licking the bowl clean, and took a long sip from his coffee.

"That fruit salad is outstanding. I loved that glaze," Alex was clearly relieved that Nick had enjoyed it, as his face lit up like the morning sun outside, "I hope I'm not prying," Nick continued carefully, "but what kind of meds did you need to take?"

Alex smile faltered slightly, but recovered quickly, "Oh, I'm fine. I just needed to take some pain medication."

Nick dropped his fork immediately and focussed intently on Alex, assessing him for injuries.

Shit! I hurt him. Was I rougher with him than I thought? Should I have provided better aftercare?

"Did I hurt you last night?" Nick was deeply concerned, but Alex didn't appear to be visibly hurt.

Alex looked confused by the question, "You mean, besides all the hickeys you left on my neck and shoulders?" he said with a raised eyebrow and a smirk. Nick immediately relaxed, "No, of course not," Alex continued, "Last night was... oh, it was amazing! I've never felt like that before in my life. No, I just need to take my pain killers most mornings. Between the scar tissue, nerve damage and my spinal injury, pain killers are a necessary evil if I want to be vaguely functional," he said, focusing on his bowl of fruit salad.

Nick didn't like the idea of Alex having to take pain killers on a regular basis. But without the benefit of knowing his boy's full medical history and needs, he couldn't really pass judgement. It was clear Alex had suffered a horrific assault at some point in his life, which had resulted in serious and ongoing medical problems. He hoped that Alex would eventually get to the point where he could open up to him and share his past experiences, then Nick could then determine if his boy was getting the care he needed. In the meantime, he would just have to trust that Alex wasn't doing anything that would cause himself more harm than good.

Nick was also relieved that Alex had apparently enjoyed what they had shared last night. He also felt a small amount of pride as he surveyed the little love bites on Alex's neck. He had marked his boy, claiming him as his own.

God, I'm such a caveman!

Nick knew the pride he felt when he looked at the little bruises was a blatantly neanderthal response, but he couldn't help but smirk at the beautiful little marks on his boy's skin.

"Why don't you try some of the omelettes. They're best eaten while still warm," Alex said encouragingly, clearly trying to change the subject to something less serious. It was early Saturday morning after all, and not the best time for heavy discussions.

Nick loaded up his plate with the strange little omelettes, which appeared to have been baked in a muffin pan, and ate a forkful of the spicy eggs. The flavour combination was extraordinary and exploded across his tongue, the chilli making his mouth tingle ever so slightly. The spiciness of the chorizo sausage was counterbalanced by the salty, creamy feta cheese. The spinach was light, sweet and almost buttery. Nick was beginning to suspect anything Alex cooked was borderline magical. He moaned his appreciation, making Alex smile wide with pride.

After a bowl of fruit salad and four of the little omelettes, Nick was stuffed to the gills. He promised Alex he would try one of the muffins later, then leaned over and kissed his boy softly.

"Finish your breakfast, then come upstairs with me. I want to shower with you."

Alex looked a little puzzled at the suggestion, but quickly finished his omelette and polished off his coffee. When Nick kissed Alex earlier, he could smell the subtle lime fragrance of his favourite shampoo, which meant Alex had obviously had a shower earlier this morning, but Nick wanted another opportunity to explore his boy's body, and also expose him to another new experience that they could share together. He took Alex's hand and lead him back upstairs.

In the master ensuite, Nick slowly stripped Alex's clothes away and folded them neatly on the vanity. He then took of his own clothes and turned on the spacious, double sized shower, making sure the water was nice and warm. He guided his boy into the opaque glass cubicle and closed the door behind them.

"Turn and face the wall, then place your hand on the tiles at head height," Nick gently ordered, "I'm going to wash you and make you feel good." Alex immediately obeyed, turning and placing his hands as instructed, spreading his legs slightly. Nick took the shower puff off the shelf and squeezed a small amount of body wash onto it. He then set about the task of slowly washing Alex all over, taking care to be gentle around his scars and spine. Alex's breathing started to hasten, moaning softly at Nick's delicate care and attention.

Nick then took the portable shower head off it's cradle, squeezed the trigger on the handle and lovingly washed away the soap suds. He then added a small amount of shampoo into his hands and gently massaged it into Alex's hair, stimulating his scalp and eliciting more pleasured moans from his boy.

After rinsing away the shampoo, Nick began to massage Alex's shoulders, laying down kisses on the back of his neck.

"You mentioned the hickeys I gave you. Did you enjoy it when I gave them to you?" Nick said softly in his boy's ear. Alex whimpered and nodded in response.

"Did you like it when I bit you on the shoulder?" Nick crooned, kissing the spot he had bitten last night.

"Yes, it was...oh...I can't describe it."

"Yeah?" Nick smiled and gently pressed his teeth around the sensitive flesh, increasing the pressure as Alex shivered and moaned with pleasure.

"You're so responsive. I like that. I can make you feel things you never imagined. Would you like that, boy? Would you like me to blow your mind?" Nick reached around and began teasing Alex's nipples, which hardened with his attentions.

"Yes, Sir, I would." Alex gasped. Nick was flooded with joy at his boy's words. He slowly ran his hands down Alex's chest, down his soft round belly, all the way to his hardening cock. He began pumping him slowly with one hand while the other gently massaged Alex's balls. Nick pressed his own cock against Alex's ass and started thrusting along his boy's crease. Alex was almost shaking at this point. Nick's plan to overload his senses with multiple stimulations was having just the affect he wanted.

"Are you close boy? Can you feel the pressure building up?"

Alex moaned and nodded, clearly losing the ability to speak. Nick was ecstatic at how he was able to bring his boy so much pleasure.

"Come for me boy, make me proud." Nick ordered, feeling his boy tense up, his orgasm only moments away. He bit down on Alex's shoulder again and his boy cried out, shooting his load all over the tiled wall. Nick clutched his boy to his chest to support him, and continued to thrust against Alex's ass. He kissed and licked at Alex's neck as he felt his own release come upon him. He growled and stiffened as he shot his load all over his boy.

"You're amazing, Alex. You are so amazing. God, I can't believe I finally found you." Nick gasped as the aftershocks of his orgasm ripped through him. He quickly rinsed them both off under the large rainforest shower head above them, then shut off the water. He lead Alex out of the cubicle, grabbed one of the large fluffy bath sheets from the towel warmer and set about the task of drying his boy. He took another towel and quickly dried himself off. He then led Alex back into the bedroom so they could get dressed.

"Do you have any plans for today, Alex?" Nick asked, trying to sound casual. He didn't want to scare Alex off.

Please say you'll stay the weekend. I want more time with you.

"Well, Saturdays I usually schedule my social media posts for the week ahead, but that only takes an hour or so. Other than that, I'm free."

"Well, in that case, why don't we go back to your place? That way you can get a change of clothes, do what you need to do, then we can spend the day together. I was thinking we might go to the markets."

Alex pulled on his shirt and jeans, "I'm not sure, I'm not comfortable going out in public much. I'm kinda breaking all my rules just being here."

Rules? What is he talking about? Why did he have rules? And why would those rules forbid him to go out? What's going on?

"Well, I thought you might like to go to the markets. There's all sorts of things for us to see and do. Plus, I remember the last time I went, they had a cake decorating stand that I think you'll love. I'll be with you the whole time. I promise, if at any point you feel uncomfortable, you just say the word and we'll leave. We can go back to your place or back here and we'll just hang out. Please, I want to spend more time with you, and I think you'd enjoy spending more time with me."

Alex appeared to ponder Nick's proposition carefully. He really hoped Alex would agree. He was having so much fun getting to know his boy, and wasn't ready to say goodbye just yet.

"Okay, maybe for a little while," Alex finally said, "The cake decorating thing has me intrigued, but I suspect you knew that would be my weakness." Alex smiled shyly.

"You'll learn that I can be very persuasive. You don't build a business like mine without knowing how to incentivise people." Nick grinned wolfishly, delighted that Alex had agreed to spend the day with him.

"In that case, maybe I should hold out for a stronger offer!" Alex said cheekily, blushing beautifully.

Nick swooped in and took Alex in his arms, holding him tight, "Is this strong enough for you?" Nick growled playfully, eliciting hooting laughter from his boy.

"You're quite the savvy negotiator yourself," Nick chuckled, "I'll clearly have to keep an eye on you, boy!" Nick kissed him deeply, then escorted him downstairs to collect the rest of his things so they could be on their way.

Chapter 13

ALEX WATCHED the streets of Melbourne flash by from the passenger seat as they headed back to his house. This was the first time he'd been in the passenger seat of his own car, and not being in the driver's seat felt so strange. Before they left Nick's house, Alex was still a little distracted because of everything that had happened over the last day or so. Who would have thought that his life would so fundamentally change in such a short period of time? But despite how amazing he felt, and how sweet Nick had been, Alex couldn't allow himself to forget the danger he was in. He needed to get in control of this situation and maintain his safety. Trouble was, every time Nick smiled at him, Alex's brain suffered a synaptic misfire and would promptly ignore that little insistent voice inside telling Alex to be more careful.

Possibly sensing Alex was slightly distracted, Nick offered to drive, and Alex handed him the keys to his little SUV without thinking. He was still feeling a little boneless from their amazing shower encounter earlier that morning. Alex would never look at a morning shower the same way again after what was easily the most mind blowing experience of his life. Nick was clearly very experienced, and knew exactly how to hit every hot spot Alex had, and even a few he didn't know he had.

Who would of thought I would get off on getting bitten on the shoulder?

The deliciously sharp sensation of pleasure/pain, that was both confusing and very arousing, made him shiver all over. Just the memory of their activities in the shower cubicle earlier had Alex's cock waking again. He shook his head and tried to pay attention to the road.

Watching Nick drive was quite an experience. The man had extraordinary focus. He was in command, clearheaded and very much in control. While Alex had realised from the beginning that this giant, muscle-bound man was a typical Alpha male, on closer observation,

Nick's naturally dominant tendencies were all the more obvious and very much on display in this moment. His insistence on driving, despite it not being his car, was a clear example of his need to be in control wherever possible. But Nick was no mindless brute. His dominating character was tempered by kindness and caring; a combination that Alex was finding totally irresistible. Nick wasn't mean or cruel. He wasn't selfish or unreasonable. Despite his dominant characteristics, he didn't see Alex as less than or inferior. They were equals. But that didn't mean Nick didn't have fun trying to get his own way. When Alex had initially refused to allow Nick to drive, Nick's response was to pout playfully, then kiss Alex's neck until he agreed to surrender the keys. Okay, that wasn't exactly playing fair, but Alex was definitely not complaining.

The closer they got to Alex's house, the more tense and anxious Alex felt. It had just occurred to him that this was the first time he had spent an entire night away from his home since he had first moved in around seven years ago.

Seven years? Had it really been that long?

"Are you alright, babe?" Nick gently asked, breaking Alex away from his inner thoughts. Nick's expression radiated concern, obviously picking up on Alex's nosediving mood.

"Yeah, it's just I haven't been away from the house for this long before. I'm worried." Alex said, noticing they were only a few streets from home.

Alex dug through his back pack and retrieved his tablet computer, "Can we pull over for a second. I need to check the feeds."

Nick smoothly pulled the SUV over to the side of the road and parked. Alex opened up the remote surveillance camera app on the tablet and carefully reviewed the feeds from each of the cameras.

"What are you doing?" Nick asked, looking slightly puzzled.

"Just making sure everything is okay." Alex muttered absently, but he immediately began to relax once he reviewed the live streaming footage and determined everything was fine. Nothing was out of place. None of the motion detectors had gone off. All the doors and windows looked fine. The property was secure. Alex let out a long breathe he wasn't aware he'd been holding on to, and the tension slowly ebbed away.

"All clear?" Nick asked cautiously, looking as if he wanted to ask why all that had been necessary, but holding his tongue.

"All clear. We can head to my place now. I know that probably seemed unusual, but I can't be too careful."

Nick started the car then pulled out into traffic, "Careful of what? If you don't mind me asking?"

Alex didn't really want to go into the details, so he tried fobbing him off by rattling off some crime statistics he'd seen on a news website. Nick was clearly not buying that explanation, but any chance to ask further questions was cut off when they arrived at Alex's house. Once the car was parked in the garage, Alex unlocked the huge iron door, closing and locking it behind them. When they got to the front porch, Alex asked Nick to remain there while he deactivated the alarm system and motion detectors. Nick complied and Alex went inside. After punching the codes into the security panel by the door, Alex gave Nick a thumbs up and Nick strolled in. Alex closed and locked the front door, placed his bag on the couch and went into his home office.

Grabbing his work laptop and his battered old note pad, he returned to the living room. Nick was still standing by the front door, apparently unsure what to do.

Wow, what a great host I am! Jeez, I didn't even offer him a drink or tell him to make himself at home. I really do need to work of my social skills.

"Please, make yourself at home. Would you like something to drink?" Alex said, trying to sound fun and welcoming, but it just came our sounding awkward.

"No, you just do what you need to do. I'll go grab myself a drink while you work." Nick said. He smiled, leaned in and kissed Alex swiftly on the lips, then headed to the kitchen, no doubt to charm my demonic coffee machine once again.

Alex found a comfortable position on the couch, set down his note pad next to him and powered up his laptop. Setting up and scheduling social media posts for the coming week was a tedious task, but it needed to be done. It helped people who followed him on his various social media accounts to discover his content, new and old, and really helped to increase his video views. As he started typing away, referring to his notes now and again, he could hear Nick in the kitchen making a cup of coffee. The damn machine was purring like a kitten again. Alex swore the devil machine hated him. Maybe it was just Nick. He seemed to be an expert in getting what he wanted, and was talented enough to encourage people (and indeed coffee machines) to conform to his will with little more than his charm and a well placed smile.

Nick soon returned to the living room with two steaming mugs of coffee, sat on the other end of the couch and handed one of the mugs to Alex.

"Oh, thank you very much. I could use a buzz. This work isn't overly exciting, but it needs to be done." Alex sipped the precious liquid and moaned his appreciation. Nick smiled wide and took a sip of his own. Alex would have to order more of those Mocha coffee pods. He added it to his 'to-do' list on his phone and returned to his work.

"So," Nick said gently, "I noticed the box of roses in the kitchen."

Alex froze, his fingers suspended over the keyboard on his laptop. Yesterday, in his haste to finish filming the cupcake video and get ready to go to Nick's house, he'd completely forgotten to put Nick's beautiful flowers into a vase. He hoped they were still okay and hadn't wilted or anything.

"Oh, I forgot to put them into some water. I've never received flowers before. They slipped my mind while I was working yesterday."

Nick's easy smile slipped a little, "Flowers from a secret admirer? Just how jealous do I need to be?" he said without heat, but more than a little trepidation in his voice.

Alex laughed, "Secret admirer? I'm not sure how secret he is!" he continued to giggle softly, amused that Nick would refer to himself that way. Nick however, was not laughing. He wasn't even smiling anymore. In fact, he looked distinctly unhappy.

Was he really that upset that I forgot to put them in water? I guess that was a little disrespectful to not treat his beautiful gift with care. Maybe I should go find a vase now? Will that make him happy?

Alex put aside the laptop and began to stand, but Nick stopped him by gently touching his shoulder, keeping him where he was.

"Who sent you those roses?" Nick said, his expression almost cold.

"Is this some sort of game? I don't really have much experience with this sort of thing," Alex asked with confusion, thinking maybe this was some sort of role playing game.

"No, it's not a game," Nick was not happy at all, "Who sent them to you?"

"You're serious, aren't you? You think someone else sent them to me? I don't understand. Didn't you send them?"

Nick looked dumbstruck. He clearly hadn't been expecting that response, obviously he had not sent the flowers.

But that didn't make any sense. Who else would send me flowers?

"Me? No! I didn't send them. Why did you think I sent them?" Nick seemed to relax slightly, but his expression was still serious.

"Well, the card..."

"What card?"

Alex got up and brought the box of roses back to the couch. He opened the lid and retrieved the small card that had been attached to the box when it arrived, and handed it to Nick.

Nick examined it and the box closely.

"I'm sorry, Alex. I didn't send these. I wish I had thought to send you flowers, but I honestly didn't know you would like that. In my experience, most men aren't big on flowers and stuff. I really am sorry. When I saw them in the kitchen, I thought perhaps you had a boyfriend and I got upset. Please forgive me."

"No boyfriend, I promise. And of course I forgive you. I would probably have had a similar reaction if the roles were reversed. But that doesn't answer where these came from." Alex said, gesturing to the box of flowers.

"If you can't think of anyone else who would send you roses, they were probably delivered by mistake." Nick suggested. Neither the card nor the box had any sender information or even a company logo for the florist.

"I highly doubt it. I don't recall ever getting a mistaken delivery in all the time I've lived in this house. Most people don't realise there is even a house here. This is really strange..." Alex trailed off, pondering where the mystery gift could have come from.

The cameras! Maybe the delivery man wore a shirt with a logo? We could find out where they came from that way.

Alex grabbed the laptop and switched on the television in front of them. He opened the surveillance camera app and accessed the DVR archive which stored all the camera footage in the cloud.

He accessed all the footage from Thursday night onward and transferred the video feed to the television's big screen. He fast forwarded until he saw two figures in the courtyard. He and Nick coming back from dinner. Once again, he noticed he'd left the iron door open, and inwardly chastised himself for not being more careful. He fast forward again through the night until he got to the footage from Friday morning.

When Alex found the section from around lunchtime, he saw the big iron door slowly open, and a man walk in holding the box of roses. Well, he didn't so much walk as he did creep. The man was wearing generic work clothes, a yellow high visibility shirt and light tan shorts. He wore a black baseball cap with a long, wide brim that obscured his face from the camera. He held his head in such a way that it almost looked like a deliberate action to avoid his face being seen. The man was wearing a pair of black leather gloves, that seemed totally out of place with a delivery man's outfit. He slowly moved across the courtyard, all the while adjusting the angle of his head to avoid his face appearing on camera. It was definitely deliberate.

Nick was watching the footage with the same laser focus he had had while driving earlier. His expression was hard, and he radiated tension.

"Do you know that guy?" He asked, his voice soft but clipped.

"I don't think so. But I can't see his face. There's something odd about him though. The way he moves..."

On the screen, the mysterious man had reached the porch. He crouched down and delicately place the box of roses by the door. He stood back up, but remained motionless. He face was still obscured. He didn't move. He didn't knock. He just stood there like a statue. He remained that way for several minutes. Then suddenly, one of his gloved hands rose, and he began slowly waving directly at the camera. Alex felt a chill run down his spine. This guy was not a normal delivery man. Delivery men don't hang around or wave at cameras. They're in and out as quickly as possible, then on to their next delivery. This guy was casual and deliberate. It was very unnerving.

"That guy is creepy. Waving like that? What the hell is he doing?" Nick muttered under his breath.

The man on the screen stopped waving. He leaned forward, knocked on the front door, turned and left quickly, once again adjusting the angle of his head to ensure he didn't reveal his face. He was out the iron door and gone. Moments later, Alex saw himself appear on the screen, opening the door and collecting the box of flowers. Alex paused the footage and sat motionless, trying to process what he had just seen.

There was something familiar about that man. The way he was so confident and sure of himself. That cocky wave to the camera. Alex's blood ran cold.

It couldn't be.

"You swear you didn't send me those flowers?" Alex asked, his voice barely a whisper.

"I swear. But I'd like to know who did. That guy gives me the creeps. I wish we could tell which delivery company he works for. You should report him for suspicious behaviour..." Nick continued to talk but Alex was no longer paying attention. A terrible thought had just run through his mind.

He picked up the card and looked at it intently. The message stood out in bold letters, their meaning finally making sense.

'Can't wait to see you again.'

OH MY GOD.

IT'S JACK.

Alex felt himself shaking all over. He was absolutely terrified. He couldn't believe after all these years, Jack had finally found him. He didn't know what to do. He was cold inside, and that made him shake even more.

"Babe, what's the matter? Are you okay?"

Alex launched himself at Nick and held him tight as he fell into a fit of hysterical sobbing. Nick returned the embrace and tried to soothe him, patting him gently, stroking his back and speaking gently to him, trying to offer comfort. Alex was too upset to understand what he was saying.

After a while, Alex began to calm himself, and Nick continued to hold him tight in those big, protective arms of his. The shaking subsided, and Alex managed to straighten himself up and take some deep breaths. He looked to Nick, who was composed and looking at him with compassion.

"Are you ready to tell me what's happening with you? Why you are so upset?"

Alex slowly nodded, as he felt he had no further reason to hide anything anymore. The damage was done. Jack knew where he was. Nick would eventually find out everything. Probably when the police showed up on his doorstep to tell him Alex had been found brutally murdered. Might as well lay it all out for him.

"So this is a long story, but it starts with a young guy named Sammy..."

Chapter 14

Eight years earlier...

SAMUEL HANSON was standing by the industrial size oven in the back kitchen of Darla's Bakery. It was mid-morning and the big breakfast rush, which usually started around seven AM, had finally died down. Since everything was under control in the shop out front, and everything was going smoothly back in the kitchen, he'd taken the opportunity to whip up a batch of the muffins he'd been experimenting with at home. He hoped Darla, who was across the street at the bank and due back any moment, would love the combination of banana and spices that made the muffins taste just like banana bread. As the muffins baked, the whole bakery was filled with the heady, sweet aroma coming from the oven. Sheila and Larissa, the two girls working out in the shop popped their heads in occasionally to praise him and beg for a taste when the muffins were baked.

He looked at the big, garish cuckoo clock on the wall to check how much longer the muffins needed.

Only a few minutes to go.

The beat-up old clock was tacky, and the cuckoo sounded like it was dying of amoebic dysentery, but Darla refused to replace it. Apparently it was a family heirloom, and had been sitting in the same place since her father opened the bakery back in the 1950's. When Darla took over in the mid 1990's, she changed the name of the bakery, but the wretched clock remained. He suspected Darla hated the clock as much as everyone else, but was too sentimental to ever throw it away.

Looking into the oven, the muffins were risen, golden and glorious. He opened the door, pulled on the large oven mitt that hung from his apron by a piece of well-placed velcro, and reached in.

"Those don't smell like blueberry, Sammy!" a sharp voice came from behind him.

Sammy startled, his hand slipping out of the oven mitt and brushing briefly against one of the super hot oven wracks. The sting of the burn was excruciating.

"Oh, Sammy! I'm so sorry!" Darla wailed, "I didn't mean to startle you! Quick, get that under running water. I'll deal with the muffins." Sammy immediately obeyed, and moved over to the huge industrial sink, putting his hand under the cold tap. The flowing water slowly took the sting out of the burn, but it was nasty. Darla turned off the oven, pulled out the muffin pan and placed it on the work bench. She immediately grabbed the first aid kit from beneath the sink and started going through it frantically.

Darla Johansson was like a grandmother to him. She was a force of nature. When it came to her business, she was no-nonsense and didn't tolerate laziness. But her gruffness was tempered by her heart of gold. She was one of the kindest, sweetest people Sammy had ever encountered. When he first applied for the job of apprentice baker when he graduated high school, he only knew a little bit about baking, and was far from being good enough, in his opinion, to actually work in a bakery. But Sammy was keen to learn, and Darla recognised this from the start. She took him under her wing and taught him everything she knew. Within a couple of years, he was a master baker and was working full time alongside Darla as they whipped up all manner of baked goods and tasty treats. Now, they weren't just co-workers, they were practically family.

When Sammy's life had been struck by tragedy just over a year ago, Darla had been there to offer emotional support. His parent's had driven out to Bushman's Pass for a night on the town, but on their way home, a drunk driver had swerved into oncoming traffic. The head on collision had killed both the drunk driver and Sammy's parents instantly. The sudden loss had been devastating, but Darla had been his rock. He would never have gotten through the pain and grief of losing his only living family if it hadn't been for the precocious old lady who refused to let him wallow away and succumb to the darkness that had flooded his world.

One day, about a month after the accident, she came around to his house baring a large cardboard box. Darla placed it down on the kitchen floor and opened it gingerly, revealing a snow white ball of fur. A sweet little kitten, who was curled up and fast asleep. Darla had been worried about Sammy being all alone in his parent's house, so she had brought him a little friend to keep him company. Sammy had instantly fallen in love with the little ball of fluff, and named him Callisto (after his favourite moon) and burst into tears. Darla had given him the time he needed to grieve, and now she was helping him to get back into a normal routine. She got him out of the house and back to work. All done with the love and dedication of a doting grandmother. Darla wasn't just his boss. She was an angel.

"It's not that bad. Just a little burn. I'll be fine."

"I'll be the judge of that young man. Now, let me get it cleaned up, and while I do that, you can tell me why we don't have any blueberry muffins today. Tuesday is always 'Blueberry Muffin Day!'"

Darla loved her schedules. Much like the cuckoo clock, the daily specials menu had not changed since her father's time, and that's the way she liked it.

"Actually, we *do* have blueberry muffins. I baked them and put them in the window while you were gossiping with Mrs Beachworth at the bank."

Darla looked scandalised, "I was NOT gossiping! That silly old goat was the one gossiping! You should of heard her going on about Mayor Willis and his new, so-called 'assistant' going away to his beach house for the weekend!"

Sammy raised an eyebrow at Darla, smirking. Darla just swatted his arm playfully and muttered something under her breath that sounded suspiciously like 'bloody smart arse.'

Once his burn had been thoroughly rinsed, dried, slathered with ointment and dressed in a bandage, Darla declared him officially healed. Sammy was tempted to ask if she would be turning water into wine as well, if she was doling out miracles, but decided against it. He thanked her and gave her a kiss on the cheek. He told her all about the muffins he had baked, then handed one over for Darla to try. He noticed the two girls from the front were none-to-subtly watching and listening to hear her verdict. She took a healthy bite and mulled it over as she chewed dramatically, drawing out the suspense.

"Outstanding!" she shrieked, giving Sammy a big hug, "These are wonderful. I want the recipe so we can add it into the big book. I think we may have just found a replacement for 'Peach Muffin Day' on Thursdays!"

Sammy was absolutely shocked. Darla had *never* once hinted that she wanted to change her menu – ever. This was unprecedented. This was like McDonald's saying 'We need to get out of the burger business and concentrate on making rice cakes.'

"Are you serious? What's wrong with the peach muffins? I make them every week and follow your recipe to the letter."

"Nothing, they're as good as always. But they aren't selling as well as they used to. I reckon these banana bread muffins of yours will be a big hit. So I'll want sixty of them baked fresh on Thursday morning. So you better look after that hand. I'll need you to show me exactly how you made them!" Darla was beaming from ear to ear, and Sammy was elated that his simple muffin recipe was responsible.

"You got it, boss! I'll get on to writing up the recipe right away," Sammy said excitedly, grabbing a battered old notebook off the shelf, Darla's recipe bible containing all the recipes used in the bakery, and sitting down at the desk in the back office.

On Thursday, the surprise change in the menu was the number one topic of discussion in town. Cooper's Landing had never been rocked by such unexpected news before, which kind of tells you just how small and boring the little hamlet was. It seemed like everyone in town had been into the bakery to see for themselves the unprecedented removal of 'Peach Muffin Day' from the chalk menu board on the wall behind the counter. The words 'Banana Bread Muffin Day' had been hastily scrawled in it's place, and everyone who came in wanted to try the new offering.

The initial sixty muffins had sold out within the first two hours, and Darla had ordered another sixty be baked as soon as possible. An even bigger third batch was baked after the second was sold out within minutes of being put in the display window. The whole day was a whirlwind of activity, as hundreds of people came in to try the new muffin. It was universally declared a vast improvement over the now retired peach muffins.

Sammy's burn still hurt a bit, but wasn't as painful as it had been a couple of days earlier. He didn't mention it to Darla, but he was certain he would be left with a significant scar on the back of his hand. Darla already felt terrible about the whole incident, so Sammy didn't want to make her feel worse. Once healed, the branding wouldn't be that much of an issue, and the occasional burn was an occupational hazard for anyone working in a bakery. That being said, he reluctantly handed his apron over to Darla when it started to throb after lunch, and he took over serving customers on the counter when Larissa went home for the day.

That was when it happened. That was when something occurred that, unbeknownst to Sammy, would change his life forever. In that moment, A handsome man walked into the bakery. Sammy knew just about everyone in town, but this man was more or less a stranger. He vaguely recognised him from Joe's Diner down the road. Sammy had been there a few days ago, dropping off their regular cupcake order, and the handsome man had been having coffee at the counter.

The stranger smiled at Sammy and stepped toward the bakery counter, his green eyes glittering in the afternoon sun. He had light brown hair, kept in a short and tidy style, and warm lightly tanned skin. His broad smile was charming.

"Hi, I'm Jacob Kennedy. Friends call me Jack. I'm new in town. Seems as though everyone around here is talking about some new muffins at the bakery. So, I thought I'd pop in and see what all the fuss was about for myself."

"Well, Welcome to Cooper's Landing, Jack. I'm Sammy. Today is the newly-Christened 'Banana Bread Muffin Day' here at Darla's Bakery. I made them myself, but we've almost sold out. So if you want one, you better be quick, or you'll miss out!" Sammy felt like he was talking way too much and way too fast. He was a blathering bundle of nerves for some reason.

What am I doing? Why would I think a guy like this would be remotely interested in me?

"Well, I wouldn't want to miss out. I'll have one muffin, please," Jack smiled wickedly. Sammy blushed and ducked down to pick up one of the muffins with a pair of tongs, placed it gently into a brown paper bag, and sealed it shut with a piece of sticky tape. He placed it on the counter, and pushed it lightly toward the handsome customer.

"Would you like anything else?"

"Yeah, how about a phone number?"

"Oh, our number is printed right on the bag under the bakery's logo."

Why would he want the bakery's number? Did he want to place an order?

"No, *your* number," Jack chuckled and smiled wolfishly. He winked at Sammy like the devil himself. Sammy blushed even deeper.

Was he serious? Was he actually flirting with me? Don't be ridiculous!

"Um, sure, I guess," Sammy managed to splutter. He grabbed a pencil and wrote his mobile number on the muffin bag. Jack grabbed the bag, handed over five dollars for the muffin and turned around.

"I'll be calling you, sweetheart," he called out as he swaggered out the door and disappeared from view. Sammy was so embarrassed.

Sheila, the other shop assistant, was gushing like a schoolgirl, "Oh my God, Sammy! He's gorgeous! I hate you so much!" she said, playfully smacking his arm.

"Don't get excited. He's not going to call me for a date. Guys like that don't go out with guys like me. He's new in town. He probably just wants me to show him around or something."

"Oh, he wants you to show him something, alright," Sheila waggled her eyebrows suggestively, then burst out laughing.

"You are shameless!" Sammy said, doing his best to look prim and proper, but he couldn't help but laugh at Sheila's ridiculous innuendo.

"What's all this cackling about? Is this the mother's meeting or something?" Darla appeared from the back room, looking puzzled at her employee's sudden jocularity.

"Sammy's got a boyfriend!" Sheila sing-songed.

"I most certainly do not!"

"He's gorgeous, Darla! He's that new guy in town. He came in and asked for Sammy's number!"

Darla scowled at Sheila, "You're as bad as Mrs Beachworth! You'd think no one had ever been asked out before!"

"He didn't ask me out! He won't be asking me out! He was just being friendly!" Sammy protested.

"Wish someone that gorgeous would be 'friendly' with me!" Sheila retorted, smirking smugly.

"Oh for goodness sake!" Darla threw her arms up in the air in exasperation and returned to the kitchen, Sammy following in her wake, desperate to escape the Sheila inquisition.

"Sammy," Darla said gently, "It's none of my business, but maybe this bloke really does like you. Why not give it a chance? I hate the idea of you being alone."

"I'm not alone. I have you. I have the girls. I have Callisto. I have my work. Being gay in a small country town isn't like being gay in the big city. I know the chances of meeting someone are slim at best. Plus, I'm not exactly the kind of guy most gay men drool over," he said patting his bulging belly, "I'm not foolish enough to believe I'm going to get some 'happy ever after'. But I have no regrets, so stop worrying."

Darla gave him a hug, "I can't stop worrying. It's my job to worry about you. Just, don't dismiss him outright. For all you know, he may just be your 'happy ever after.'"

To Sammy's surprise, Jack called that night and asked him out to dinner the following evening. Since the only restaurant in Cooper's Landing was Joe's Diner, it was either that or drive two hours to Bushman's Pass, the nearest big town. The diner sounded good to Sammy, and they agreed to meet there at seven.

Big city marketing companies could learn a lot from small Aussie country towns. Nothing got word around faster than the gossiping residents of Cooper's Landing. A few years ago, Old Mrs Clyde had mentioned to her neighbour in passing that her roof was leaking. Within hours, a dozen tradies descended on her house, all offering her a free quote.

If the people of Cooper's Landing got excited over the announcement of a new flavour of muffin at the bakery, the news of a real life homosexual date at the town diner was the story of the century. Somehow, within an hour, everyone in town had heard about the upcoming date. Sammy wasn't concerned per se, since he'd never really had any problem with overt homophobia or bigotry amongst the townsfolk. He occasionally heard a few muttered words now and again, usually from the older people or super religious types. But on the whole, the town was fairly accepting. That being said, the idea of two men having a first date at Joe's Diner was apparently something of a news sensation, and everyone wanted to see this once in a millennium event first hand.

Since Sammy only lived a few streets away from the diner, he decided to walk there on Friday evening. Friday nights at the diner are usually pretty quiet. But this Friday night however, was anything but. It seemed like the whole town was there. As he approached the diner, Sammy saw every parking space was taken, and rows of cars were parked on both sides of the street. The diner's busiest day was never *this* busy.

Jeez, don't these people have lives? This is insanity!

Sammy should have seen this as a sign that the evening was going to be a disaster. But, being a fairly open minded and positive individual, he swallowed his nerves and entered the diner, spotting Jack at a small booth at the back. The entire diner fell silent as he slowly walked towards Jack, who was smiling, but looking more than just a little confused at the town's reaction. As he made his way to the booth, a few people gave Sammy smiles, a thumbs up or the occasional 'Go get him, tiger!' - all of which made Sammy feel like a new animal being introduced to a zoo enclosure.

"Hi, Sweetheart!" Jack stood and hugged Sammy in greeting. Sammy thought this was a bit forward for a first date, especially with a huge audience, but shrugged it off, figuring Jack was probably nervous too.

"Hi Jack. Sorry about all this," Sammy gestured towards the people in the diner, most of whom were trying unsuccessfully to *not* look like they were looking at them, "The people of this town are... whack jobs."

"I must admit, I wasn't expecting all this attention, but they all seem to be really friendly. I've had so many people wishing me luck with our date."

Sammy cringed, "Oh, God! I've had the same thing too. It's like we're front page news!"

The two men settled in the booth and a waitress came over with menus and, in what had to be a first for Joe's Diner, a candle in a silver holder. She placed the candle on the table, lit it with a match and scurried away. Sammy couldn't believe how ridiculous this evening was getting, but surrendered to the madness and just chuckled along with Jack as they decided on what they would order.

It didn't take long for Sammy to determine his first ever date was a big fat bust, and it had nothing to do with the crowd of slack-jawed gawkers watching every move they made.

For one thing, Jacob 'friends call me Jack' Kennedy, was an obnoxious bore. Jack made no attempt to ask Sammy any questions about himself or to engage him in conversation. Instead, Jack spent the entire date talking about himself. When ever Sammy attempted to contribute to the conversation, Jack would quickly cut him off, often speaking over his date, in favour of telling yet more stories about himself. Sammy also noticed that at some point, Jack had started referring to Sammy as his 'boyfriend' - a lot.

Now, Sammy didn't have much experience with dating, but even he thought this was a little unusual, but was never given the opportunity to correct his date, since there was never enough of a lull in the incredibly one-sided conversation to interrupt.

The evening reached peak insanity when, over dessert, Jack literally declared his undying love for Sammy and seriously suggested they should move in together. It was then that Sammy finally stood up, thanked Jack for the 'pleasant' evening, and attempted to make a hasty departure, saying that he needed to get home to feed his cat. A lame excuse, but honestly the best thing he could come up with on the fly.

Jack rushed ahead of him to open the diner door for him, apparently trying to be gallant and romantic, then insisted on walking Sammy home. Sammy tried to protest, but Jack was having none of it. Sammy was thankful it was a short walk to his house, suddenly very eager to bring this terrible night to a swift conclusion.

When they arrived at his house, Sammy once again thanked Jack, said goodnight and tried to unlock his front door. Before he even had the chance to slip the key into the lock, Jack slammed Sammy up against the door and began forcibly kissing him with a bone-shuddering clattering of teeth, his hands everywhere. Sammy tried to resist, but Jack was strong and forceful. He was momentarily stunned by the unexpected assault, but quickly regained his senses and immediately found the strength to shove Jack away, knocking his date to the ground. Sammy could taste blood in his mouth from where Jack had bitten his lower lip. He told Jack to leave and never to call him again and promptly went inside, slamming the door behind him and locking it up tight. Sammy immediately took a shower, so thoroughly disgusted by his sleazy date's appalling behaviour, and brushed his teeth several times.

He went to bed, Callisto curled up asleep on the pillow next to him, and tried to get some rest. So much for Darla's theory of 'happy ever afters.'

The next few days at the bakery were surreal, to say the very least. From open to close, the shop was filled with townspeople desperate to find out how Sammy had enjoyed his date, when the next date would be and, most bizarrely, if 'wedding bells' were in the air. The people of Cooper's Landing were sweet, but needed to be immediately institutionalised.

While Sammy didn't tell anyone about what Jack did after their date, (he didn't want to be responsible for a Frankenstein-esque chase with flaming torches and pitchforks) he simply told people that the date had not gone well and that he wouldn't be going out with Jack again.

This disappointed and confused everyone. Disappointed, because they all apparently genuinely wanted to see Sammy happy and settled; and confused, because Sammy's claims that the date hadn't gone well seemed to be massively contradicted by the sheer number of gifts, teddy bears, bunches of flowers and romantic helium balloons that were being delivered to the bakery every few hours. All from Jack. All with twee little notes attached continuing to declare his love and begging for another date. The whole thing was beyond over-the-top and completely out of control.

When Darla insisted on knowing what the hell was going on, and after some initial resistance, Sammy finally gave in and told her everything that happened on the date. By the time he had finished telling her about the violent kiss on his doorstep, Darla was fuming.

"You should have him charged with assault! That rat bastard should be rotting in jail!" she shrieked in the back office of the bakery, and Sammy hoped the girls out the front hadn't heard.

"Shhhh! He got out of line and I stopped him. There's no need to get the police involved. Not that they'd do anything about it anyway. But these presents and balloons and texts are getting out of control. I don't know what to do."

"What texts?" Darla asked, "Is he sending you naughty sex pictures on your phone?" she sounded scandalised.

"No! No, nothing like that! In the last three days, he must have sent me over a hundred text messages. All telling me he loves me and wanting to meet up for another date. I already told him never to call me again..." Just then, his phone dinged, signalling the arrival of yet another text from Jack, "Here we go again, this is getting ridiculous!"

"He's insane! Seriously, Sammy. That's not normal behaviour. He sounds like one of those crazy stalkers. I think you need to text him again, state clearly that you don't want to be contacted by him again and that you don't want to date him. If he continues, I think you might have to bite the bullet and get the police involved. This can't go on." Darla said, looking around at the dozens of gifts that now littered the back of the bakery.

"I know, but I don't know how sympathetic the cops are going to be. Most people in this town are fine with me being gay, but everyone knows the local police are all part of the church set, and their opinions on homosexuality are well known."

"This is criminal behaviour, Sammy!" Darla shouted, "What ever their personal opinions, they have a job to do. They have to enforce the law. Send the text to Jack. If it continues, I'll go with you to the police."

"No, Darla. That won't be necessary. I can handle this on my own. I appreciate all your help, but some things you just have to sort out for yourself. I'll send the text now," Sammy started texting rapidly, "There, done."

Sammy vainly hoped that would be the end of it. But he was dead wrong.

The next day, the torrent of gifts stopped abruptly. The text messages continued, thought. Only now, Jack wasn't declaring his love. He was angry, abusive and would send cruel, hurtful messages day and night. Eventually, Sammy just turned off his phone. He rarely used it anyway, so it wasn't a big loss. This only escalated matters. Soon, Jack started coming into the bakery directly, demanding to see Sammy. When Sammy politely asked him to leave and repeated he didn't want to see him any more, Jack would cycle between looking like a kicked puppy and seething with resentment.

"You're a selfish, ungrateful little bitch!" he boomed, scaring the hell out of Larissa and Sheila, who immediately joined Sammy in telling Jack to leave. Darla threatened to call the police if he didn't get out of her bakery immediately, and Jack reluctantly left, still screaming obscenities. Sammy still resisted going to the police, convinced that eventually Jack would get the message, lose interest and move on. But that was not to be.

That night, Sammy got home from work and kicked off his shoes. Usually, Callisto would come scampering into the hallway and insist on being picked up and petted, but he was nowhere to be seen. Sammy looked in his bedroom, the lounge room, and the kitchen, but the little kitten was missing. Then he noticed the back door was open. He was certain it was closed and locked when he left this morning.

Cooper's Landing was hardly a criminal hotbed. The worst the local police usually had to deal with is breaking up the occasional drunken fight down the pub, or people speeding on the highway. Most people didn't even bother to lock their doors. But Callisto was something of a little furry Houdini, and had figured out quickly how to leap up and dangle off a doorknob until the door opened. So locking doors had quickly become essential in order to avoid any unsupervised escape attempts.

Figuring Callisto had gotten outside into the backyard, Sammy went to retrieve the little fuzzball, but froze when he noticed the damage to the door jam. Someone had kicked the door in. Suddenly seized with panic, Sammy grabbed his father's old cricket bat that he kept by the backdoor and began searching the house more thoroughly. When he reached the bathroom, the only room left to be checked, he got a sinking feeling inside. Something was terribly wrong, he could feel it in his bones. Sammy opened the bathroom door and nearly collapsed when he saw the lifeless corpse of his sweet little cat hanging from the shower rail, his entrails dangling from a jagged wound on his belly.

Sammy screamed and dashed out of the house and ran to the neighbour's house. Thankfully Mrs Lucas was home and she called the police immediately.

Later that evening, Sammy was still at the local police station being interviewed about the break in. Sammy told them everything. He told them about the date with Jack, the ongoing harassment, the gifts, the texts, and his threatening behaviour at the bakery. But it was clear the local cops were not buying a word of it. They made ridiculous remarks about how Sammy should be 'flattered to have found another poof in town' and even went so far as to accuse him of murdering his own cat for attention.

Sammy was furious, but somehow managed to maintain his calm and finish writing out his official statement. The officer in charge of the case claimed he would look into everything very carefully, but this didn't bring any comfort to Sammy, considering their minimal investigations so far couldn't even identify Jack's home address or place of work.

Typical small town cops. They simply don't give a shit.

Sammy was under no illusions. This case would be quickly buried without any serious investigation. They had absolutely no intention of looking into this matter, and if Sammy persisted in pushing for a proper investigation, he would only end up antagonising the already annoyed cops who would have no second thoughts in trumping up some nonsense charges against Sammy rather than waste any of their supposedly valuable time looking for Jack. He'd known this would be a waste of time, but it's not like he had anyone else to turn to for help.

Once he was cleared to go home, Sammy walked back to his house to see the forensic officer in the front yard packing up to leave. When Sammy asked if it was okay to bury Callisto now, the officer insisted on taking the kitten's body 'for evidence.' But Sammy couldn't help notice Callisto had been unceremoniously dumped into a cardboard box, rather than a plastic evidence bag. The officer offered a lame apology, but the smirk on his face as he dumped the box in the back of his car made it abundantly clear he wasn't remotely sorry. Just a cheap, petty act of cruelty from another small-minded man. As the officer drove away, Sammy burst into tears, unable to hold back the grief and frustration of the whole situation.

Sammy went inside and secured the property as best he could. The backdoor could no longer be locked, and it was too late at night to call someone out to repair it. He'd have to deal with it in the morning. He wanted to shower, but couldn't bare to go into the bathroom, the room still stained with Callisto's blood. He quickly changed his clothes and settled on the couch in the living room. He was too upset to sleep. He considered calling Darla, but it was late and they both had an early start in the morning. He curled up on the couch and tried to rest, eventually slipping into a dreamless sleep.

During the night, Sammy awoke to a strange sound. It sounded like a scraping noise coming from the kitchen, but when he sat up, he couldn't hear anything, and dismissed it assuming it was a dream.

"We are meant to be, Sammy" a voice whispered in the dark.

Sammy immediately woke up, confronted by the image of Jack standing over him, a kitchen knife in his hand. Sammy was paralysed with fear.

"What the fuck are you doing here? Get out!"

"Oh, don't be like that sweetheart. This playing hard-to-get is getting very tiresome." Jack purred, an evil smile on his face.

"You killed my cat! Why? Why would you do that?"

"I won't let anything stand in the way of our love!"

"You're insane! Get out of my house! I'm calling the cops..." Sammy stood up and reached for the phone, but Jack struck him with the back of his hand, knocking him back on to the couch. Sammy cried out in pain.

"You ungrateful little slut! After everything I've done for you, you treat me like this? You don't deserve my love!" he roared.

Sammy tried again to get up, but Jack was too quick. He plunged the knife into his chest, agonising pain blooming between Sammy's ribs as the knife sliced through flesh and scraped against bone. Sammy screamed and tried to defend himself, but Jack kept stabbing him over and over, even as Sammy fell forward and tried to crawl away. Jack plunged the knife into his lower back twice and Sammy stopped moving.

"No escaping now, my love. We're going to be together. Whether you like it or not..."

Sammy felt like he was floating. He could see the whole scene before him. His prone, broken body on the floor. Jack looming over him with the bloody knife in his hand. His head was swimming. His body felt cold. The room began to spin and the world went dark as he plunged into oblivion...

Sammy groggily opened his eyes. The light was bright. Everything was white and fuzzy. He couldn't focus on anything clearly.

I'm dead. I'm in heaven. My life is over.

"Just relax Mr Hanson, we're taking care of you." a soft voice said.

"Are you God?"

"Nah, mate. I'm an ambo. You're on your way to hospital in an ambulance. Try to stay calm. We'll be there soon."

"They have hospitals in heaven?" Sammy didn't understand, but didn't get a chance to hear God's explanation. He fell back into the darkness and everything went black.

When Sammy woke up again, the light was subdued. He was sore all over and he couldn't move. He thought he was strapped down to something, but he could see his limbs weren't restrained. He found, with some difficulty, he could move his arms, but his legs wouldn't respond.

"Mr Hanson, you're finally awake!" a bright, bubbly voice said. A young woman dressed in white came strolling into the room.

Hospital. I'm in a hospital. What had happened? Oh, Jack. Oh my God, JACK!

"Just relax. You're perfectly safe. You've been unconscious for nine days. Do you remember what happened to you?" the nurse asked softly.

Nine days? How can that be correct. I was in the ambulance a few minutes ago.

""Yes," Sammy croaked out, his throat dry and sore, "Can I have some water, please?"

The nurse brought him a small cup of ice chips, "Now, try a few of these. Nice and slow. You don't want to make yourself sick."

The sweet relief of the ice chips melting in his mouth and the cool water slipping down his parched throat was heavenly.

"Thank you. Jack stabbed me. He tried to kill me. Where is he?"

"I don't know, Mr Hanson. The police were here earlier asking if you were awake. Two of your friends are standing guard outside. I'm sure they would love to see you. And the police probably have a lot of questions about what happened to you. I'll call them shortly to let them know you're awake."

"Please call Darla. Darla Johansson. She'll be worried sick about me. Let her know I'm okay."

"You just sit back and relax. I'll take care of it. In the meantime, I'll tell your friends to come in if you like?"

Sammy nodded weakly, his strength ebbing away with the exhausting task of chewing ice chips. Moments later, Sheila and Larissa walked in, their faces drawn with grief.

"Sammy!" Sheila grabbed his hand and gave it a reassuring squeeze, "We thought we'd lost you. How are you feeling?"

"Sore, tired. I can't feel my legs."

Larissa held his other hand and squeezed it too, "You're lucky to be alive. I'm so sorry this happened to you. No one has seen or heard from Jack. The whole town is looking for him. The cops are finally taking the case seriously. Your neighbour, Mrs Lucas, saved your life. She heard your screams and called the cops. She ran straight over to help you, but Jack ran off before the cops arrived. He's been MIA ever since."

Jack is missing? Damn. I was hoping he was arrested and locked up.

"Is Darla okay? She must be in such a state, worrying about me. I probably scared her half to death."

The two women looked at each other and shared a pained expression.

"What? What is it?"

"I'm so sorry, honey. I hate to be the one to tell you this," Sheila said, her voice barely a whisper, "Darla passed away a few days ago."

Sammy's world collapsed in pieces all around him. He couldn't process what she had said. Everyone he loved, everyone he considered family was now dead.

"The shock of what happened was too much for her. She had a heart attack when the police came to the bakery to tell her about your stabbing. She collapsed on the spot. We tried to resuscitate her, but..." Sheila trailed off, but Sammy still couldn't believe what he was hearing. He tried to hold himself together, but the tears slipped down his face and the two women joined him. They comforted each other until Sammy was too weak to speak, and he slipped into am uncomfortable sleep.

After three months of surgeries, physical rehabilitation and more examinations than he'd care to remember, Sammy was finally cleared to leave the hospital. He was left with multiple scars on his body, none of which could be repaired without extensive cosmetic surgery. Sammy had gone through enough surgeries, and didn't want any more. He also had a permanent spinal injury. He could finally walk again, but the nerve damage to his lower spine meant he was in constant pain, walked with a limp and would frequently lose muscle control in his legs leading to falls. Armed with a sturdy walking cane to help keep him stable, he slowly made his way out of the hospital, and was driven home by Sheila. Not that his home would be of any comfort to him.

Sheila explained to him that in the wake of his stabbing, word had gotten around town that Sammy had approached the Police for help with Jack's stalking. When they found out he had effectively been refused help for what appeared to be purely homophobic reasons, all hell broke loose in Cooper's Landing. The townspeople were furious that the Police could so callously disregard the safety of one of the citizens they were supposed to protect and serve. Even the Mayor had made an official complaint to their superiors and demanded an official enquiry into the conduct of the officers in Cooper's Landing.

The people of the town had gotten together to repair the damage to Alex's house, replaced the locks and installed a simple alarm system, in the hopes of making Sammy feel safer when he eventually came home from the hospital. Unfortunately, Sammy didn't feel like he would ever feel safe in that house again.

With no living relatives, Darla had left everything, including the bakery, to him in her will. But due to his injuries, he was in no fit state to run a full time business involving such heavy labour. With both bakers gone, he was was left with no alternative but to close the bakery and put the building up for sale, which broke his heart. Mayor Willis immediately purchased the old bakery building for a fair price, adding it to his extensive property portfolio and Sammy was glad to have one less thing to worry about. Sheila and Larissa took new jobs at Joe's Diner, so at least they would be okay.

Thanks to the funds from the sale of the bakery, the payout from his parent's life insurance policies, their inheritance and his own savings, Sammy had more than enough money to live comfortably for the rest of his life. But what would his life be now? He had no job, no family and the certainty that his physical injuries were unlikely to get any better than they currently are. But just when Sammy thought his situation couldn't get worse, it did.

A few weeks after leaving the hospital, Sammy started receiving threatening text messages from an unknown number. It didn't take a genius to figure out who sent them. Unfortunately, the police identified the number as being a burner phone, and thus untraceable. Despite their deepest sympathy for his situation (probably inspired by a healthy dose of guilt for not believing him when he initially came to them for help) there was little they could do. The small police station simply didn't have the same resources as a big city cop shop, and it's not like they could stand guard over him 24/7. They suggested Sammy stay with family, but since he didn't have any family left, that suggestion was moot.

Sammy knew Jack would be back. He knew he had no hope of defending himself in his current state. He had no alternative. He had to get away. He had to disappear and never come back. As much as it would hurt to leave everyone and everything he knew, it was the only way to ensure his survival and elude Jack. Sammy had always dreamed of running away to the big city, but he never thought he would be doing it under circumstances like these. He started formulating a plan, and set about making it happen.

A few days later, Sammy's plans were in place, and he prepared to put it all into action. He started by taking the long bus ride out to the next town, Bushman's Pass, and went to the local courthouse. He couldn't risk doing any of this in Cooper's Landing. Not if he wanted it all to remain secret.

Once off the bus, he went into the courthouse and set about legally changing his name to something generic that couldn't be traced back to him. He transferred all his money and assets into new accounts and set about changing and updating everything with his name on it. Within a few hours, Sammy Hanson no longer existed, and Alexander Michaels walked away in his place.

It would take Alex a while to get used to his new identity, but if all went according to plan, he wouldn't be in Cooper's Landing long enough for it to matter. While he was in Bushman's Pass, he went into the local Real Estate agent and put his house on the market. He gave the agent carte blanche to do whatever she needed to do to sell the house as quickly as possible, and she agreed to handle everything. She would arrange for his furniture and personal possessions to be collected and donated to charity, then hire a cleaning firm to prepare the house for market.

He then went to a nearby rental car dealership, and hired a large SUV with more than enough storage room for the personal items he just couldn't bare to leave behind. Once the lease paperwork was signed, Alex tossed his phone in a nearby rubbish bin, drove himself back to Cooper's Landing and immediately set about loading the car with his clothes, laptop, a few personal items and locked up the house.

He pinned a handwritten note to the door, explaining to anyone who stopped by that 'Sammy' had gotten a job offer in Perth, and had been forced to move at short notice. The note left a brief farewell to his friends in Cooper's Landing and thanked them for all their support. Alex hoped this red herring would throw anyone off his scent long enough for him to get to Melbourne and hidden away. Once in seclusion, there would be no trace to follow and Alex would be free to start his quiet new life.

He looked at the home he had grown up in. The house he had lived in all his life. He knew this would be the last time he would ever see it. Sammy carefully bent down and put the keys under the welcome mat at the front door, then got into the car.

As he drove away and began the eight hour journey to Melbourne, he thought about the little house he had bought only a few days earlier. It was tucked away in a little laneway and surrounded on all sides by big concrete walls. He'd found it online and bought it sight-unseen. From the photos, it needed a lot of renovations, but he would sort that out when he got there. His biggest priority right now was getting away from town unseen and getting himself into seclusion. Jack wouldn't be able to kill him if he couldn't find him.

The long drive was painful, his back throbbing the whole way, and Alex was damn near crippled by the time he found the little laneway and got the car locked up in the dilapidated old garage. He'd return the rental car to the nearby dealership in a few days. He quickly discovered the house was in a terrible state of disrepair, but would do until he could organise a contractor to come around and begin work on renovations. He had very specific plans for his new home, with the biggest priority being security. He curled up on the floor in the large empty living room, and drifted off to sleep.

The next few days were spent drawing up a list of requirements for his new home, researching security systems and looking up contractors to make it all happen. Alex had plenty of money to get the job done, so the only concern was how long it would all take to complete, and where he would stay while the work was happening. Alex eventually decided to rent a small high rise furnished apartment in a nearby secure building.

Over the coming months, the neglected little house, tucked away in a quiet laneway where nobody could see it, underwent a remarkable transformation. The exterior walls surrounding the property were left untouched. They were structurally sound and any cosmetic alteration would just draw attention. The outside brick walls of the house were rendered with concrete, then painted a dark grey. The roof tiles and gutters were repaired, replaced or cleaned as required. The windows were replaced with modern frames and new locks added. Then each window was fitted with solid steel security bars. The small front yard was converted into a low maintenance courtyard featuring a covered outdoor sitting area, paved front porch and some large potted plants to break up all the stone and concrete. The garage was fixed up and a new automatic security roller door installed.

As for the interior, the whole house was more or less gutted. New hardwood floors, new bathroom and the two smaller bedrooms were converted into one large main bedroom. The remaining bedroom would serve as a home office. Plain painted walls and muted tones throughout. Nothing fancy, just neat, tidy and comfortable.

The kitchen was the crowning glory. Alex had a plan on how to fill in his days, so he designed a kitchen that was not only be functional as an everyday food preparation area, but could also serve as a filming space. A large lighting rig was installed on the ceiling, extra wide bench tops were added and all the best domestic appliances were used. Alex didn't want to skimp on the kitchen appliances, as he would need reliable fixtures that would stand the test of time.

All in all, it took almost three months to complete the work. The last job was to install the extensive security systems. Surveillance cameras, motion detectors, back to base alarm monitoring and more. Once it was all finished and secure, Alex was free to move in full time.

He would always remember the first time he walked into his newly refurbished home. Although he had visited several times during the renovations, this was the first time since the saw dust was cleared, the paint dried and the furniture in place. He sat down on the plush new sofa in his brand new living room, and breathed a sigh of relief.

He was safe. He was hidden. He was home.

Chapter 15

ONCE ALEX had told Nick his story, he felt emotionally drained. But strangely, he also felt like a weight had been lifted off his chest. Carrying the poison of his past for all these years had weighed him down a lot more that he had realised, and it was a relief to finally let it go slightly.

Nick had held him tight, stroking his hair and soothed him gently as Alex had relayed the details of meeting Jack Kennedy, the horrors that had followed, and his subsequent need to disappear. When he was done, Nick continued to hold him tight.

"Thank you for trusting me, for sharing your story with me. I know how hard that must have been for you to do, but I promise you don't have to worry anymore. I will keep you safe."

Alex was quite right to be sceptical. Nick was an amazing man, but somehow he doubted his hunky new lover had much experience in repelling bloodthirsty psychopaths.

"If Jack has found me, the best thing for me to do is disappear again. If he can't find me, he can't…"

"NO! You will not be running away," Nick said with absolute finality, "We don't even know if this actually *is* Jack. It could be just some random delivery guy who came to the wrong address. Yes, the footage is a bit creepy, and maybe it really is him, but before you change your name and move to Timbuktu, perhaps we should contact the police and get their opinion?"

Alex didn't like the idea of getting the police involved. Last time, they'd been less that worthless and all but stood by and allowed Jack to nearly kill him. Alex had no reason to trust they would help now.

"I know what you're thinking, but this is Melbourne, not some one-horse town in the middle of nowhere. The police here will take you seriously and they'll investigate properly. Copy the footage onto a thumb drive and we'll take it to the police station. Then pack a bag. You can stay at my house for a few days while we sort this out. While you do that, I'll pack up the roses and the card. Maybe the police can get fingerprints or DNA from them."

Nick spoke with clear authority. He was in charge, making plans, and taking the burden off Alex's back. Normally, Alex would find this kind of behaviour a little presumptuous, even obnoxious, but with Nick it was enormously comforting. He was Alex's strength when he needed it most. Nick was calm when Alex wanted to scream and fall apart. In that moment, he realised Nick would never hurt him. Nick would always be on his side. But above all else, Nick genuinely cared. In that moment, Alex started to realise what true love was. He was witnessing it, and he was feeling it within himself. His long frozen heart had begun to thaw.

Alex did as instructed, transferred the security footage to a portable storage device, then packed some clothes and a few personal items. Once he had everything he needed, Nick took his overnight bag along with the packed up flower box to the car, while Alex set the security alarm and locked the doors. Once in the car, Nick in the driver's seat, Alex felt the tremors of fear slowly dissipate. With Nick on his side, he could do this. He could face the police. He could stay safe. For the first time in years, Alex had a life worth fighting for. He wasn't going to let Jack or anyone else rob him of everything that he had worked so hard to build. He wasn't going to be a victim anymore.

Several hours later, Alex and Nick were still at the police station talking with a detective. Nick had been right, they took everything he said seriously. They reviewed the security footage and agreed there was something very odd about the mystery man's behaviour. They sent the flowers and card off for forensic examination. Detective Paul Kincaid, a large and intimidating man in his early forties, made it clear that it may take several days to get the DNA and fingerprint results. Apparently, it wasn't like on television, and the results didn't come back in a few minutes. In the meantime, he would be checking with surrounding buildings to see if they had CCTV cameras installed so they could compare the footage. This may garner a lead to the identity of the delivery man.

The detective also suggested Alex consider staying with friends or family if he felt unsafe at home. Before Alex could respond, Nick stated matter-of-factly that Alex would be staying with him until further notice, and when Alex suggested he would only need to stay a few days, Nick made it clear he was welcome to stay as long as he needed; his tone of voice brooking no argument. The detective's eyebrows rose at Nick's proclamation, but relaxed when he saw Alex had no objection to Nick's somewhat dictatorial nature. The detective smiled knowingly, then asked Alex to begin filling out his written statement.

The full official statement, covering everything, including Alex's time in Cooper's Landing, his former identity, everything he could remember about Jack, plus everything related to the incident with the flowers, took forever to write out. Nick, loyal and dedicated, sat patiently by his side the whole time. He never once complained about spending part of his weekend in a police station. He just offered his support, a kind word or a steadying hug when things got too emotional.

When it was all done, the detective promised to be in touch, gave Alex and Nick his contact details should they need to contact him for any reason, and walked them out to their car. Stepping out into the street, Alex suddenly realised the day had flown by, and that it was now early evening. The sun was all but set, and the first twinkling stars were beginning to appear in the inky purple sky.

Nick suggested they pick up something simple for dinner on the way back to his house, then they could spend the evening unwinding and relaxing. Alex thought that was an excellent idea, but was still very much preoccupied, thanks to the long and winding trips down memory lane he'd been forced to undergo today.

Usually, he avoided thinking about Jack and his past life in Cooper's Landing. But today it had been necessary to put his discomfort to one side and let it all out. Now that he had, he wasn't sure he could get the lid back on his emotions. Alex was afraid that, despite his earlier hopes of taking control of his life and not being a victim any more, his opening of all these old wounds might make that task a great deal more difficult than he had initially anticipated.

After stopping at a little Chinese restaurant to pick up dinner, a selection of deliciously fragrant dishes that Nick must have ordered ahead of time while they were still at the police station, the two men headed back to Nick's house and sat down at the kitchen table to eat. Nick served out the food onto two large plates while Alex went and washed up in the downstairs bathroom.

When he returned to the kitchen, dinner was ready along with two big glasses of lemon iced tea. Alex and Nick sat down to eat. Nick was clearly ravenous, as he devoured his meal in record time, while a distracted Alex picked at his food, not really tasting anything.

"Everything okay?" Nick asked softly.

"Huh? Oh, yeah, it's delicious. We'll be eating leftovers for days."

"Actually, I meant are *you* okay? You look like you're a million miles away."

"Yeah, it's just..." Alex wasn't sure how to put how he felt into words, "Today has been a bad day. Thinking about everything I've been through, having to go over it again and again. It's left me a little... I don't know..."

"Distracted?" Nick suggested, "I'm not surprised. But it's over for now. How about we finish our dinner, and then I'll take you upstairs and try to take your mind off it," he said with a slightly wicked grin.

"Really? You can take my mind off all this?" Alex said with hopefulness.

"I can help you to relax, distract you from all those bad memories and make you feel amazing. Just trust me and let me take care of you."

"I trust you completely," Alex said without a moment's hesitation, "Please help me. After everything today, I'm finding it hard to focus on anything but the past."

Nick rose from his chair and held out his hand to Alex, who immediately took it and stood up. Nick led him out of the kitchen and up to the master bedroom. Alex put himself entirely in Nick's capable hands and allowed his lover to take care of him. He offered himself completely to his lover, knowing he could trust him completely. Nick stripped off Alex's clothes, slowly and carefully, then quickly removed his own. He pulled back the bedcovers and led Alex to the bed, instructing him to lie face down.

Alex was in a significant amount of pain. The tension from the day had caused all the muscles in his back to spasm and contract, leaving him uncomfortable and wound up. Nick, apparently picking up on his lover's discomfort, was prepared to deal with this. He went into the ensuite bathroom for a moment, then returned with a small bottle in his hands.

"This is massage oil. When I rub it into your skin, it will warm you up and help to release all the tension in your muscles. A nice, long, full body massage will do you wonders and make you feel amazing. All you need to do is relax, give yourself over to me, and allow me to take care of you. I will make you feel better, boy. Trust me."

"Yes, Sir," Alex whispered, relaxing immediately at the sound of Nick's firm voice. Having Nick to help shoulder his worries and tension was the most extraordinary experience. So many years of having to be strong and in charge, it was a relief to relax and let someone else take the reins, even for just a little while.

Nick poured the rich, fragrant oil into his hands, rubbed them together briefly, then started smoothing it all over Alex's back. Once he was slicked all over, Nick started at Alex's feet. Slowly working the tension out of each muscle and tendon. No pressure, just gently coaxing the muscles to relax and unwind. He slowly worked his way up Alex's legs, thighs, buttocks and hips. Every inch was smoothed and caressed, Alex groaning as he felt the day's worries and pains melt away like ice cream.

Nick clearly had extensive massage experience. Alex had only had a few massages as part of his physiotherapy after the spinal surgeries, and they definitely didn't feel like this. Every inch of his skin was sensitised, every muscle was wrangled into submission. The more Nick worked his tired, painful muscles, the more Alex found it difficult to focus on anything but Nick's tender touches. He had never felt so relaxed. When Nick ordered Alex to roll over onto his back, Alex was so at peace, he didn't even worry about the oil possibly staining the sheets. He just did as Nick instructed and submitted to his lover's touch.

Nick then started again, this time doing everything he had just done to the front of Alex's body. More oil was applied and every inch of skin was caressed and touched, except for his cock. Before Alex could ask why, he got his answer. While Nick was gently teasing Alex's now very sensitive nipples, he felt his cock become incased in hot wet heat. Nick was lovingly sucking him from tip to root, all the while stimulating Alex's nipples. When Nick moaned around his cock, he felt a vibration in his balls he'd never experienced before. Nick didn't stop, he just kept bobbing up and down, slowly ramping up the suction and swirling his hot tongue around Alex's cock head. He couldn't think. He couldn't speak. All he could do was feel and moan. When his cock hit the back of Nick's throat, he thought his heart was going to stop. The sensation was intense. Like electricity in his blood. Nick increased the speed of his suction, pinching his nipples and making Alex cry out incoherently. When Nick chuckled at his boy's reactions, the deep vibration it triggered inside made Alex's balls draw up. He couldn't stop it now, his orgasm was barrelling toward him, and his whole body was on fire with desire.

When Nick took him down to the root, holding him in his hot tight throat, Alex felt his cock pulse several times as he shot load after load into his lover's mouth. His mind was shattered by the exquisite over-sensation of it all. He lost all capacity for rational thought, just tumbled wordlessly into a pleasure coma. His eyes closed and his world melted away, safe in the knowledge that Nick had kept his word. He'd made him forget about the day's events. He'd made him lose his mind altogether. He fell into a deep, relaxed sleep.

Chapter 16

AS NICK expected, his intensive full body massage had done the trick. His boy was completely relaxed, the sexual release had pushed him over the edge and allowed him to drift off to sleep, safe and warm in Nick's bed. He lay next to Alex for a short time to ensure his boy was deeply asleep, then quietly slipped out of bed, put on his robe and headed downstairs to make some phone calls.

Nick had been deeply disturbed by Alex's revelations earlier that day. He'd known his boy had suffered a horrific trauma, but the details were so much worse than anything he'd imagined. The stalking, the attempted murder, the death of his boss. The whole series of events must have been unbearable. Only to have the harassment start again, with no real hope of stopping it.

No wonder Alex felt he had no choice but to run away and hide from the world.

Having to walk away from everything you know and live in almost total isolation was something Nick couldn't comprehend. The agonising pain and unrelenting fear Alex must have experienced was beyond imagining. All these years living alone, afraid of being near other people for fear of being spotted in a crowd. Alex's slightly eccentric social skills now made perfect sense. Nick was hopeful that now he knew the truth of his boy's past, he could help to break down those defensive walls around him and help him to regain a normal life. But first he would need to convince Alex that hiding was not the answer.

Nick wasn't sure if the delivery man in the surveillance footage was in fact Jack, but even the slightest possibility of Alex being in danger needed to be taken seriously. Nick had been furious when he heard of the callous disregard the Cooper's Landing Police had displayed when Alex had approached him for help. The shear incompetence and mean-spiritedness of their handling of Alex's case was downright criminal. He wanted to find out if anything came of the Mayor's complaints and demands for an official enquiry into those events. Nick was tempted to get his legal team to investigate what action, if any, could be taken against the Cooper's Landing Police. But any such action would have to wait for the time being. There were more immediate matters that needed to be addressed.

Nick grabbed his phone off the kitchen table and called his assistant, Andrew. It was early Saturday night, but the current situation required prompt action to ensure the safety and security of his boy.

"This better be good. It's Saturday night!" Andrew answered with mock surliness.

"I have a situation and I need your help." Nick used his serious 'business' voice. His tone was clipped and brooked no nonsense. Andrew clearly picked up on this and immediately fell into professional mode.

"What's happened? Are you okay?" the tone of his voice conveying genuinely concerned.

"I'm fine, but I need to upgrade security at my house and at Alex's house as soon as possible. I want surveillance cameras installed inside and outside of my house, and I want a top of the line alarm system too. I want Alex's alarm system upgraded to the same standard. I'll email you his address," Nick knew from experience that Andrew would already be taking short hand notes as he spoke, so he didn't need to repeat himself or slow down.

"Has something happened? I'll need to brief the security company to make sure they install appropriate equipment. Is there a specific threat?"

"Alex may have a stalker. The individual is likely to be armed and should be considered extremely dangerous. The police are involved and investigating as we speak. In the meantime, I want to make sure both our properties are secure and monitored. Also, I want two security guards, one for each house. They are to be armed and remain in place until further notice. I want them ready and in position by morning. Don't worry about the expense, I'll cover it all. Use my company expense card and I'll have my accountant sort it all out later."

Nick could hear Andrew scribbling furiously, making sure he had all the details. Andrew was nothing if not efficient. He knew he could rely on his assistant to get everything sorted out.

"Anything else you need?"

"Yes. Cancel all meetings and appointments for the next few days. Reschedule where possible. I don't want to leave Alex alone until we get this situation under control."

"Understood. I'll get on it right now. I'll be in contact if I need any further information or if there are any problems. Stay safe and don't worry. I've got everything in hand."

"Thanks Andrew. I can't tell you what this means to me. You're a lifesaver."

"That's what I'm here for. Email me Alex's details so I can get started, and call me anytime if you think of anything else you need. Goodnight, Nick."

Nick ended the call and opened the email app on his phone. He quickly typed in Alex's address details and sent it off to Andrew. He then sent an email to his company's Accounts Manager, informing her that there would be some unusual transactions in the coming days, and to coordinate with his personal accountant to ensure everything is recorded properly and all bills settled. Finally, he sent an email to his housekeeper, instructing her not to come around until the property had been secured.

Nick scolded himself for not addressing his home security sooner. It was something he had always intended to do, but it had never seemed like a priority. At least the house was relatively secure. Heavy doors with expensive, high end locks. The windows were all lockable and the exterior had several sensor lights. It wasn't perfect, but it would have to do for the moment. The security guards would be in place by morning, and hopefully the security system would be installed later that day.

With everything sorted out for the time being, Nick tidied up the kitchen, washed the dishes and put away the leftovers from dinner. He then grabbed Alex's overnight bag off the couch in the living room. But before he could do anything, the peaceful silence in the house was shattered by a bloodcurdling scream from upstairs.

Alex. Alex is in danger!

Nick dropped the bag and ran up the stairs. He burst into the master bedroom and switched on the light, but there was no one there but Alex. He was still asleep, but clearly in the middle of a horrific nightmare. The twisted look of anguish on his boy's face broke his heart, and he dashed to the bed to comfort him. Alex was writhing under the bedclothes, scrambling to defend himself from an invisible attack. Nick wrapped his arms around his boy and held him close, trying to soothe him.

"It's okay, Alex. It's just a bad dream. You're safe with me. No one will hurt you, I promise."

His words were a healing balm to Alex, and he began to calm immediately. He settled and his eyes opened. He started mumbling apologies, but Nick assured him there was nothing to be sorry about. He spooned in behind Alex and held him to his chest. Nick smoothed his hands up and down his boy's chest and belly. Alex murmured quietly and closed his eyes, quickly returning to sleep. Nick leaned in and kissed the back of Alex's head, closed his eyes and was soon drifting off to sleep himself. He would stay by his boy's side all night to keep the nightmares away.

Nick and Alex enjoyed a lazy sleep-in on Sunday morning. Nick ended up gently waking his boy shortly after nine, and they started the day with another sensual morning shower. Nick loved exploring Alex's body; lovingly caressing his smooth pale skin; finding all those little spots that made his boy moan with pleasure.

Once showered and dressed, they went downstairs to the kitchen and began putting together a light breakfast. Alex wanted to cook something more elaborate, but Nick planned on getting his boy out of the house today, and what better excuse than Sunday morning brunch at the markets? They eventually sat down at the kitchen table, sipped coffee and grazed on muesli with dried apricots and cranberries, topped with greek yoghurt.

"I thought I should let you know," Nick said casually, "I'm having security cameras and a new alarm system installed here as soon as possible. I'm also upgrading the alarm system at your place. I've also arranged for security personnel to patrol both properties until this whole situation in under control."

Alex held his spoonful of muesli suspended in midair, "Um, when did you organise all this?"

"Last night. I got my assistant onto it after you went to sleep. He'll get it all sorted out."

"Well, get your assistant to email me copies of all the bills for the security at my place, and I'll sort out payment," Alex said before returning to his breakfast.

Nick wasn't sure how to approach this. He knew that Alex wouldn't be able to afford the kind of system Nick had in mind, let alone the 24/7 security guards. Alex may once have had a lot of money from his inheritance, but given Melbourne's notoriously expensive property market, the combination of the move to the city and the fact Alex hasn't held down a full time job in almost a decade must have seriously hit his savings.

"You don't have to worry about paying for any of it. The alarm system and security patrols will be very expensive, and I'm sure it will be outside of your price range. But I don't mind covering it. It'll give me peace of mind knowing you're safe."

Alex started laughing, his mouthful of muesli inelegantly spraying out of his mouth, making him cough and splutter.

Why is he laughing? Doesn't he believe that I'll keep him safe?

"Are you joking?" Alex said, trying to rein in his laughter, "Out of my price range? You're serious?"

"Well, I know you had to have spent a lot on the move to Melbourne, and I figured since you haven't been able to work a normal job for a long..."

Alex cut him off mid-sentence, "Um, you do realise I'm not poor, right? Far from it. I can afford a security system."

"Yes, but you may not be able to afford the kind of..."

"Nick, I make around $50,000 a month."

Nick was gobsmacked.

Alex made that kind of money? From cupcakes? I'm in the wrong bloody business!

"Between advertising revenue, video distribution deals, sponsorships, product placement deals and cookbook sales, I'm more than comfortable. A top of the line security system isn't going to break the bank."

Nick had seriously underestimated Alex's business prowess. He knew his boy had a massive online following, but he had no idea that would translate to such a successful business. Maybe he should start listening to his social media manager instead of tuning her out when she starts going on about online engagements and audience reach. Nick made a mental note to set up a meeting with Sarah to get caught up on what could be done to improve his company's online presence.

"I had no idea. Wow, I thought the whole cupcake thing was a hobby. I didn't realise you were a full-blown media mogul! I apologise for being so presumptuous."

"Apology accepted. You aren't the first person to make that mistake. The number of companies I've dealt with who don't have a clue how the online world works is astonishing. But, they're quickly realising that traditional media is underperforming and new media is the future. Luckily for me, I got in on the ground floor and have managed to build a nice little business for myself. So yeah, send those invoices through to me and I'll get them sorted out."

Alex smiled, finished his breakfast and took his bowl dishwasher. He then made himself another coffee and returned to the table.

"So," Nick said, "I was thinking we might go out and get some fresh air today. We didn't get to go to the markets yesterday, but we can go there today. We could have a wander around, have some brunch, maybe grab some stuff for making dinner tonight. What do you say?"

"Okay. I'll just go take my meds, then I'll get my stuff together and I'll be ready to go," and with that, Alex headed off to the bathroom.

Nick smiled. Spending the day with his boy was going to be great, but spending it out of the house would be even better. Hopefully this would be the first step in getting Alex out of his shell, and more importantly, that prison-like house he's been hiding in for all these years.

Nick's phone started ringing, the caller ID showing his assistant's number.

"Hi Andrew, anything to report?"

"Bad news, I've spoken to every security company in the city, and the earliest anyone can install the security cameras and alarm systems is Wednesday."

Nick groaned with frustration, "Offer them more money. I want everything installed by tomorrow afternoon."

"It's not a question of money, Nick. I already offered them more to expedite installation. The reality is every company is booked solid and there is no one available to work at such short notice. I tried some smaller companies, but none of them could offer the kind of top-of-the-line systems you wanted."

"Would it be feasible to hire independent contractors to work with the security company to do the installations?" Nick was quickly running out of ideas, and he wanted to make sure both houses were secure as soon as possible.

"I already considered that, but most of this work requires specialty training, and even if it didn't, it would take a few days to find contractors and organise for them to be briefed on how to install the systems appropriately. If you're seriously worried about your safety, perhaps you should consider finding somewhere more secure to stay for a few days. A hotel perhaps?"

"No, I'm not sure we need to do that just now. It's annoying we can't get everything done immediately, but with the security guards in place soon, we should be fine for the time being."

"If you think that's best. But let me know if anything changes, and I can make arrangements. I took the liberty of calling my friend at the Royal Park Hotel, and he's keeping a suite aside for you just in case."

"How the hell did you manage that?" Nick was stunned. The Royal Park was the most exclusive hotel in the city. Bookings were rare as hen's teeth.

"He owes me a favour. So just call me if you need the suite and I'll arrange everything. Oh, before I forget, the security guard is in place at Alex's house, but he can't access the property as the main entry is locked. You'll need to drop over a spare set of keys so he can check everything and properly secure the property. The guard for your house should be arriving shortly. They'll have a shift changeover every twelve hours."

"Thanks, Andrew. Tell them we'll drop the keys off shortly. I promise there will be a big bonus for you this month for all this extra work you're putting in."

"I'll hold you to that. Just stay safe and call if you need anything."

Nick thanked him again, then ended the call. Alex returned from the bathroom, pocketed his phone and wallet, and was ready to head off.

As they prepared to leave for the markets, there was a sharp knock on the front door. Alex froze in place, but Nick assured him it will be the security guard they discussed earlier. Sure enough, when Nick answered the door, a large man in a dark suit and security lanyard around his neck introduced himself. Nick quickly briefed him on the layout of the house and backyard, gave him a set of keys, then left the guard to his duties.

"Ready to go?" Nick said, smiling and holding his hand out to Alex. His boy returned the smile and took his proffered hand. They headed out to the car and left for the markets.

Chapter 17

IT HAD been many years since Alex had been out in such a crowded public place. In fact, he wasn't sure he had ever been in such a crowded place. The hustle and bustle of thousands of people wandering around the markets was overwhelming to say the least. Just trying to find parking in the enormous outside carpark had Alex's head spinning.

The Queen Victoria Market, located in the north of the city, was a Melbourne institution. For over a century, the people of the city had come to the market stalls, situated under a series of large open ended sheds, to buy fresh fruit and vegetables, fresh fish, clothes, local artisan goods, tourist souvenirs and more. Alex knew this from Googling the markets on the drive over from Nick's place. He'd imagined a small market with a few stalls. But the reality was a massive indoor/outdoor retail experience. Crowded and noisy and bursting with activity. When Nick found a parking spot and switched off the car, Alex was trying to remain calm.

"This place is huge!" Alex said almost breathlessly, "I'm not sure how I'm going to go, getting around a place this big."

"Don't worry, babe," Nick said reassuringly, "There are plenty of places to stop and sit if you need to take a break. Plus, we're not going to go to the entire market and see every single stall. We'll just grab some stuff for dinner, then take a quick look at a few stalls I know you'll like. If you need to stop and rest, just say the word and we'll grab a seat. There's quite a few cafes, bench seats and little restaurants too, so we won't be short of pitstops."

Alex relaxed a little. With his spinal injury, mobility was a serious issue. But he trusted Nick knew what he was talking about. The crowds and the noise, however, were making Alex anxious. Being in such an open, exposed place was very dangerous. What if Jack was here, laying in wait? Alex wasn't sure this was a good idea.

"I promise, it's going to be okay. I'm here, and I'm not going to let anyone hurt you. But if you really want to go, I'll understand."

Alex knew all he had to do was say the word, and Nick would turn the car around and take them home. But Alex was curious about the cake decorating stall Nick had mentioned the day before, plus he could use another cup of coffee. Also, with a big, muscly protector by his side, Alex probably didn't have anything to worry about. He smiled at Nick and stepped out of the car.

The produce shed was on the far end of the market from the carpark, but Nick knew a shortcut that allowed them to walk straight through the middle, while also giving them plenty of places for Alex to stop and rest along the way. Their destination was worth the journey. The enormous fresh food section was astonishing. The dozens of stalls featuring every conceivable fruit and vegetable, along with vendors shouting out the days specials, was unlike anything Alex had ever experienced. The waves of people rushing around him was initially very overwhelming, but soon Alex got into the swing of things. The smell of fresh fruit, the crowds of shoppers and the sound of jazz music playing from a band busking on the street nearby was a glorious cacophony of sights, sounds and sensations.

Nick had a couple of large, reusable shopping bags with him, which were quickly filling up with a variety of vegetables for a big stir fry he planned to make for Alex that evening. One of the vendors offered Alex a sample slice of the most delicious looking mango, and the sweet yellow flesh was delectable. He grabbed four and added them to the shopping bag. They would make an excellent dessert tonight. At the end of the shed was a variety of artisan stalls, featuring locally produced honey, jams, candles, soaps, organic produce and more. Alex couldn't resist buying a pot of creamed honey and a bottle of apple dessert wine.

"The next section is my favourite," Nick said with a grin, pointing towards a doorway at the end of the shed, leading into a small brick building, "This is the deli hall. Several little hole-in-the-wall shops offering freshly made smallgoods, bakery items, hot food, hand crafted chocolates, freshly roasted and ground coffee…"

"Sold!" Alex cut him off, "What are we waiting for? I could use some coffee after all this walking and shopping," he said with a giggle. Nick smiled widely, clearly enjoying his day out.

The deli hall was a small, enclosed space with dozens of small shops clustered together around a circuited pedestrian walkway. The hall was crowded, but Alex was immediately drawn to the aromas of all the amazing local foods on display. One shop sold various cheeses, another sold an array of dips, pesto sauces and freshly made yoghurts. But the enticing aroma of roasting coffee beans had Alex almost floating on air to a little shop around the corner.

Nick and Alex sat and enjoyed freshly brewed espressos, complete with chocolate pistachio biscotti, then set about getting the rest of the ingredients for dinner. Nick also grabbed some fresh Turkish bread while Alex grabbed some ham and Swiss cheese from the shop next door. Together, they had everything they would need for dinner tonight and lunch tomorrow.

Once they had all the food items they needed, Nick escorted Alex out of the deli hall and headed towards the other market sheds. They strolled slowly up a row of stalls featuring clothes, toys and kitchenware. Nick directed him to a small stall tucked away in a corner. Several tables were laid out offering a wide variety of cake decorating supplies. Nick had not been exaggerating. This stall was Alex's highlight of the trip. Piping nozzles, cake tools, and lots of decorating gadgets were on display, and Alex was in heaven. He spotted a fancy airbrushing tool being demonstrated by a young woman with multicoloured hair and large black-rimmed glasses. Alex watched as she carefully sprayed a fine mist of blue food dye onto a plain iced cake, and marvelled at the beautiful painted effect on the white fondant. Alex was tempted to buy an airbrushing kit there and then, but decided to leave it for another day. That didn't stop him from grabbing a few new piping nozzles and a set of fondant tools that he could easily see himself using in his videos. Nick watched on with a giant grin on his face, clearly very pleased with himself.

"Okay, I admit it, the cake decorating stall is amazing. Thank you for bringing me here. I've had a marvellous time."

"You're very welcome. Now, is there anything else you want to get?"

Despite having plenty of places to stop and rest, Alex was starting to get very sore from all the walking. Nick had been very patient in allowing him to stop and rest whenever he needed to, but Alex needed a proper chair to sit in and let his back relax for a while. Plus it was getting close to lunchtime.

"Could we find somewhere for lunch? I could use a longer break before we head home. Somewhere with comfortable chairs, perhaps?"

"No problem. There is a great little Turkish cafe around the next corner. It has great coffee, great food and lots of chairs. Give me your shopping bags and we'll head over there now," Nick said, holding his free hand out to receive Alex's random collection of purchases.

The outdoor seating at the cafe was comfortable and in the perfect position to catch the light cooling breeze that blew through the market sheds. They enjoyed freshly made pides and rich Turkish coffee, neither of which Alex had tried before. The coffee was super strong but really nice. He'd be buzzing for hours!

Alex looked around the fairly quiet dining area, then moved in closer to Nick, "Can I ask you something?" he said, his voice a low whisper.

"Of course, you can ask me anything."

"When we... um..." Alex was so embarrassed to ask, "When we are... together... you know, in bed..." he could feel himself blushing hard.

"Yes?" Nick said with a sly, wolfish grin.

"Well, are you always so... um... bossy?"

Nick's wolfish grin was now a super wide smile and he chuckled softly, "Yeah, most of the time. I can't deny I enjoy being in charge in the bedroom. I've always been a bit dominant. But I get the impression you enjoy it when I take control."

Alex was sure his face was now on fire. It must be the caffeine making him talk about this in such a public place.

"You don't have to be embarrassed about it. We're both consenting adults. What we do in bed is nobody's business but our own. As long as were both enjoying what we do for each other, that's all that matters."

Alex pondered this for a moment. It's not like anyone else would find out that he enjoyed being submissive in the bedroom. There wasn't anyone else to find out. He'd always enjoyed his fantasies involving large alpha men taking control of him. Alex just never thought it was something that would actually happen. But now he had Nick, and he trusted him to keep him safe. Maybe he could ask Nick to try something with him.

"So," Alex said quietly, looking around again for eavesdroppers, "If I wanted to try something, we could talk about it?"

"Absolutely," Nick reached out and held Alex's hand, "A relationship is all about communication. Feel free to talk to me about anything you want or need. If it's something we may both enjoy, I don't see why we couldn't try it. But this is probably not the best place for such a discussion."

Alex nodded in agreement. They settled down and leisurely finished their lunch. Once Alex's back had been given a chance to relax for a while, they made their way back to the car, loaded their shopping and departed the markets.

Just as they pulled out of the carpark, Nick's phone rang. He answered the call on the car's handsfree system.

"Nick Hawke," he answered curtly.

"Mr Hawke, this is Clint Alsop, the security guard at your home. There has been an incident. I have alerted the police and they are on their way."

Alex froze.

Had Jack found Nick's house? Was the security guard hurt? What was going on?

"What kind of incident?" Nick asked, bristling with tension.

"There's been some minor property damage. The assailant didn't gain access to the house though."

"We're on our way. We'll be there shortly."

Nick ended the call, then focussed on driving. Traffic was reasonably light for a Sunday afternoon, so there shouldn't be any major delays.

"What do you think has happened?"

"I have no idea. But I want to get back as soon as possible. Hopefully it's nothing too serious. Maybe the security guard is overreacting. Don't worry about it for the moment."

Easier said than done.

Soon, they were pulling into Nick's driveway. The police were already there, with a throng of officers standing near the front door. One of them was photographing something, but Alex couldn't see what it was from the car.

As they approached the front of the house, the crowd dispersed slightly, allowing them to see what the police were focussed on. Something had been attached to the front door. As they got closer, it became clear the object was a large kitchen knife that had been stabbed into the large wooden door.

Alex gasped when he got close enough to see the full scene. He could hear his blood rushing through his ears, and he could feel his heart pounding against the inside of his ribcage. He could barely breathe and his mind was seized by an overwhelming blanket of pure fear. Any lingering doubts Alex may once have had about who the mysterious delivery man was had now been swept away by the tableau displayed before him.

The powerful, stainless steel blade had been used to pin a small piece of paper to the door like a macabre thumbtack. When Alex got close enough, he felt the blood drain from his face when he recognised the paper as a playing card.

The last thing Alex saw before his knees went weak, he lost his footing and passed out was the eerie smiling face on the playing card.

The Jack of Hearts.

Chapter 18

NICK MANAGED to catch the collapsing Alex before he hit the ground. He swept his boy up into his arms and tried to comfort him. Alex had been so brave today, venturing out into the world for the first time in years, but the shock of seeing the ghoulish display of a knife jammed into Nick's front door had clearly been too much for him.

After a few moments, Alex shakily awakened, and Nick helped him inside the house via the back door, leaving the forensic officers to their work. He carefully escorted his boy to the kitchen table and helped him into a chair, then Nick went to the fridge to retrieve a chilled bottle of water.

"Here, take some small slips, nice and slow. You've have a bit of a shock, so try to relax and take it easy for a little while."

"Relax?" Alex spluttered on the mouthful of water, "How am I supposed to relax? He's going to kill me! He knows I'm here. He knows about you. What the hell am I going to do? This is all my fault. I should never have left the house."

Alex began to softly sob, and Nick was at his side in a moment, bringing him into a gentle embrace.

"Hey, it's going to be alright. He's not going to hurt you. We're going to sort this out together. None of this is your fault. So don't go blaming yourself for this sick bastard's behaviour."

Nick had to admit, he hadn't been initially convinced that the mysterious delivery man in the security video *really* was Jack. Alex had been in paranoid hiding for so many years, jumping at shadows and locking himself away from the world. Nick understood Alex's reasons for this, but up until this point, Nick had been thinking this may simply be a case of Alex's prolonged isolation having blurred the lines somewhat; making it hard for Alex to be sure what was a genuine threat and what was *perceived* to be a threat. But this latest development could not be so easily dismissed, and Nick now found it impossible to believe that anyone other that Alex's stalker could be responsible.

"But if I had just stayed in my house, none of this would have happened."

"You're right. None of this would have happened. We would never have met. We would never have got to know each other. We would never have discovered we had common interests. We would never have enjoyed Movie Night together. We would never have connected so deeply. God, Alex, I care so much about you. I swear, I will do everything possible to keep us safe. I'm not running away and neither are you. You are worth staying and fighting for. I won't let Jack or anyone else scare you back into hiding."

Alex buried his face in Nick's shoulder and hugged him tighter. They stayed there for several minutes, just holding each other. Nick doing everything to give his boy comfort and reassurance that everything will be okay in the end.

A short time later, the security guard and Detective Kincaid entered the kitchen from the back door. Nick and Alex sat down at the kitchen table and invited the two men to join them. The detective pulled out his notebook and pen and flipped to a blank page so he could presumably take notes as he questioned them.

"Before we begin," Kincaid said, "Mr Michaels? Do you require medical assistance?"

"No, I'm fine now, thanks, "Alex said shakily, "It was just a bit of a shock. I'll be okay."

"Good, are you feeling up to answering some questions?"

Alex nodded and, when the detective asked him about their movements today, Alex gave a detailed account of their trip to the markets, then their trip home.

"Thank you Mr Michaels. I'll need you both to come to the station to make an official statement, but that can wait until tomorrow. For now I'd like to know what happened while you were both out of the house," he said, turning to the security guard, who stiffly introduced himself as Clint Alsop.

"Well, I arrived to begin my patrol just shortly before the two gentlemen left for the markets. I went inside and checked all the windows and doors to ensure they were secure, then returned to my main position by the front door. I circuited the building at random intervals and checked the backyard to ensure everything was undisturbed. Shortly after one PM, I did another circuit, and when I returned to the front of the house, the knife was in the door. I didn't see anyone around. No vehicles. Nothing suspicious. I phoned it into the police, then I called Mr Hawke to inform him of the incident. There was no suspicious activity before the first responders arrived."

Detective Kincaid scribbled down the details in his notebook, "Mr Hawke, does your home have security cameras?" the detective asked.

"Not yet," Nick replied with slight frustration, "I'm currently trying to get some installed, but there has been a delay. I'm hoping to have them installed sometime in the coming week."

"I'll ask your neighbours if they have cameras. It's possible one of them may have captured footage of the assailant. Maybe his vehicle too, if he had one."

Nick had to admit, Jack had balls to pull something like this in broad daylight. It may be a Sunday afternoon, and this may be a quiet neighbourhood, but his willingness to strike with a security guard on duty plus God knows how many possible witnesses in the surrounding houses, clearly showed Jack was not afraid to take huge risks. This attack seemed to be somewhat reckless, which meant Jack was even more dangerous than Nick had already thought he was, since there was no way to predict what he would do next.

Turning to Alex, Kincaid flipped through his notebook to a page of hastily scribbled notes that Nick couldn't decipher. He wondered idly if even the detective could read them.

"Mr Michaels, this morning I was able to get in contact with the Cooper's Landing Police. They sent through their case files, but there wasn't much to go on. Their investigations didn't appear to be too detailed."

"Yeah, I figured they wouldn't be. The local cops made it clear they weren't that interested, at least until I got stabbed." Alex said bitterly.

"Well, according to the files, they attempted to locate Jack Kennedy in the days after your assault, but despite extensive enquiries around town, they were unable to determine his home address, his place of work or his current whereabouts."

"So he just disappeared?"

"Given the lack of initiative on their part, I doubt the local police would ever have found him. I used the information you supplied in your statement to run a search for Jack Kennedy in all our databases. I found nothing. No birth records. No bank accounts. No driver's licence. No tax file number. Zip. He was obviously using a false identity. I'm really hoping one of your neighbours has recorded some security footage, otherwise I don't have much to go on at this point."

Nick frowned. He was deeply disturbed by this revelation. If Jack was using a false identity, there may be no way of tracking him down. He'd hoped that the police would be able to locate this lunatic quickly and bring him in. But now that was looking like an impossible task, and it would make protecting Alex all the more difficult.

"I would also like to point out, we have no real evidence so far that this 'Jack' is even involved in these latest events. For all we know, this could be totally unrelated to Mr Michael's stalking and assault."

Alex shot out of his chair like a rocket, his face ablaze with barely contained rage, "No evidence? Are you fucking serious? His name is Jack! There was a Jack of Hearts pinned to that door with a fucking kitchen knife! How much more evidence do you need?"

Nick stood and ran his hand up and down Alex's back in a soothing motion, "Calm down, we're going to figure this out."

"Calm down? I'm not going to calm down! Last time they told me there was no evidence it was Jack, he did this to me!" and with that, Alex wrenched up his shirt to reveal the multiple scars left by the stabbing. He turned to make sure the detective got a good look at the jagged marks. The detective paled briefly, but quickly schooled his features.

"Last time, he stabbed me nine times and left me to bleed out. This time, he won't stop until I'm dead. So don't fucking tell me to calm down."

Alex collapsed back into the chair, the energy from his outburst draining away as he softly keened, his head in his hands.

"Mr Michaels, I want you to understand. I'm not saying I don't believe you. We are going to do everything we can to catch whoever is responsible for this. All I'm saying is that, at the moment, we don't have enough evidence to draw any specific conclusions. I'm working hard to gather as much information as I can, so I can find this guy and keep him away from you."

Alex slumped, allowing his hands to fall into his lap, "I'm sorry, I didn't mean to lose it. It's just... I'm scared. I know what he's capable of. I know what he'll do if he gets to me."

"He's not going to get to you. He'll have to get through me first." Nick growled, showing Alex he was not going to be intimidated by anyone.

"I know, that's what I'm afraid of."

Nick was momentarily stunned. Alex was afraid for Nick's safety. He couldn't remember the last time someone was worried about him. The revelation tugged at Nick's heart and made him fall for Alex just a little harder.

"I understand you have hired security guards for both your homes, but until the alarm systems and cameras are installed, it might be a wise precaution to spend a few days somewhere else, at least until everything is secure." Kincaid suggested.

"My assistant can arrange for us to spend a few days in a hotel. They have excellent security and we can be there before nightfall. We can even make the bookings under false names."

"I'd recommend against staying anywhere that's can be accessed by the general public, or by anyone wandering in off the street. Hotels have security, but you'd be safer in a private residence."

"What about your house, Alex?" Nick suggested.

"But he already knows where I live."

"True, but your house is like Fort Knox. It has alarms, motion sensors, cameras and even bars on the windows. Plus we have a security guard in place already."

"I guess," Alex said, "But maybe it would just be easier for me to disappear again. I could go somewhere he'd never find me."

"No," Nick said with blunt finality, "Running away isn't the answer. You'll be running and hiding for the rest of your life. Always looking over your shoulder, wondering when Jack was going to reappear. Now we have the police involved, it's only a matter of time before they find something that will let them find Jack and put him behind bars. We just have to hunker down and wait until we get the all-clear."

"You're right," Alex said with conviction, "I can't keep running. Last time, I ran because I had nothing to stay for. Now I have you. I won't let Jack ruin this. I care about you, and I don't want to hide forever, alone and unloved. I need to see this thing through."

Nick brought Alex into a tight embrace, not caring about the two other men in the room. Clint looked away, clearly uncomfortable with the open display of affection. Kincaid smiled ever so slightly, but his eyes looked longingly at the couple. Nick suspected the detective didn't have anyone special to go home to.

"Are you sure you want to do this, Nick? I would understand if you wanted out. I wouldn't hold it against you. This kind of drama must be a real turn off."

"I'm not going anywhere. I spent years looking for the man of my dreams and, now that I've found him, I'll be damned if I'm letting him go. I'm in. I'm all in. Let's pack up everything we'll need for the next few days, then we can head over to your house."

The detective rose to his feet, "I'll arrange one of the uniforms to escort you. Remember, if you think of anything relevant, or if anything suspicious happens, don't hesitate to call me. Day or night. I want to catch this guy and get him off the streets."

Kincaid and the security guard left the room via the back door. Nick locked it behind them, then the two of them went upstairs to begin packing.

Chapter 19

ONCE AT Alex's house, the two men set about securing the house. Every door and window was checked. The security alarm was set. The big TV in the living room was set to display the various camera feeds in and around the house. The only movement was from Russell, the security guard stationed outside in the courtyard.

As they wandered around the house double checking that everything was secure, Alex cast his mind back over the events of the last few days, comparing how he felt now against how he felt seven years ago in the wake of Jack's stabbing attack. Alex couldn't deny he was just as scared, but compared to seven year ago, he felt a lot more confident now. This change was down to one thing: Nick.

Given the insane amount of drama and danger Alex was bringing into their lives, most guys would have run for the hills by now. Not Nick. He had made it clear, time and time again, that he wasn't going to be chased away. He was here to stay the distance. He genuinely cared about Alex.

Alex had read many trashy romance novels during the long years of his self-confinement. Almost all of them had the theme of love at first sight; characters falling head over heels madly in love with each other in, what Alex had always considered, an utterly ridiculous time frame.

Who really falls in love with someone so quickly?

Alex's parents had frequently said that they knew they would end up getting married as far back as their first date. Alex had always figured this was simply his parents looking back at past events through rose coloured glasses. But everything that had happened to Alex over the last few days forced him to wonder if there wasn't more truth to their remembrances than he had initially thought.

There was no denying the attraction between Alex and Nick. While they initially seemed to be very different people with very different lives, it didn't take long to discover they had a lot of similarities too, and their differences complimented each other, so much so it almost seemed as though they were made for each other by design.

While Alex wasn't convinced about the concept of love at first sight, he definitely felt something for Nick. The more time they spent together, the more his feelings grew. It also seemed those feelings were mutual, if Nick's refusal to walk away for his own safety was anything to go by. Alex wasn't sure he was ready to call these feelings 'love' just yet. They had only known each other a few days, after all. But for the first time, Alex actually felt like such a thing was possible. Which was easily the biggest change in him since he was forced to leave Cooper's Landing all those years ago.

Once everything was secure, Alex instantly began to relax. Whether it was because they had locked themselves away from the outside world, Nick's stabilising presence or just being in familiar surroundings, he couldn't be sure. But the anxiety and nervousness that had plagued him most of the day had finally started to dissipate. But he was still on alert. Jack was out there somewhere. He knew where they were. It was only a matter of time before he made his move. But Alex needed to put that out of his head for the time being. For now, there was nothing else he could do but sit and wait.

Alex's realisation about his feelings for Nick, regardless of what he wanted to call them, filled him with confidence. He had wanted to ask Nick something at the markets, but his shyness and reservations, coupled with being in such a public place, made it hard to bite the bullet and ask. Even now, with it just being the two of them alone in his house, he was still nervous. What he had to ask was big. He wasn't sure how to broach the subject.

Maybe now isn't the time? Maybe take things slowly and see what happens?

"So," Alex turned to Nick, who was sitting beside him on the big couch in the living room, "What should we do now to pass the time?"

"I know what I want to do." Nick said with a lascivious grin, his eyes ablaze with heat.

""Really? I guess I could break out the old Scrabble board..." Alex said teasingly, desperately trying to keep a straight face.

"Not quite the kind of game I was thinking of..." Nick growled playfully, moving himself closer and leaning into Alex's neck to nibble that sweet spot that always set him on fire.

"No Scrabble? How about Snakes and Ladders? Monopoly? Tiddlywinks perhaps?" Alex tried not to laugh, but couldn't stop his giggles from escaping. He also tried to maintain his composure in spite of Nick's ministrations, with about as much success. Nick bit down sharply on Alex's shoulder, growling deeply as he did it, and the vibration shuddered through Alex's body. He could no longer hide how turned on he was, and he moaned with pleasure at the full body sensation.

"Not a fan of board games, huh?" Alex laughed as Nick ran his fingers under Alex's shirt, seeking out his nipples and gently plucking them as he continued to work the sweet spots on his neck and shoulders.

"I think you know what kind of games I like to play, boy." Nick said with that low, sensual baritone that made Alex shiver. He idly wondered if Nick could get him off just by talking dirty to him in that tone of voice. Alex wanted to try that one day. His man had a wonderfully dirty mouth.

"Well, I don't know about you, but I've had a bit of a stressful day, and could use a nice long soak before we do anything else. Why don't you join me?" Alex stood up and offered his hand to a slightly puzzled Nick. He then led Nick into the big bathroom just off the main bedroom.

"Wow, that spa bath is massive!" Nick said, staring at the embarrassingly large tub that Alex had had installed when he renovated the house.

"Yeah, it's a little over the top, I know. But with my back, I needed something to help loosen up my muscles, and I had the space for it."

Alex turned on the water and added some foaming bath oil, then turned his attention to his handsome lover.

"I think you're a little over dressed for the tub, Mr Hawke. But I think I can help you with that," Alex said with a cheeky grin. He reached forward and began attempting to remove Nick's dark leather belt.

"Mr Michaels, are you trying to seduce me?" Nick said, biting his lower lip with a barely contained gleeful smile.

"I'm giving it my best damn shot." Alex grumbled under his breath as he tried to undo the buckle, which stubbornly wouldn't come loose.

"Wow, I'm not used to this. Usually I'm the one doing the seducing." Nick said, carefully moving Alex's hands and helping to undo the buckle himself.

"Oh, am I doing this wrong?" Alex blushed, "Did you not want me to..."

Nick kissed him deeply to cut him off. His hands clasped Alex's head on either side to keep him from moving, then gently released him, motioning for Alex to continue undressing him.

"No, it's just different. It's good to change things up now and again."

Alex smiled shyly, then continued stripping Nick of his clothes until he was naked. His powerful body on display for him, a glorious study in masculinity. The wide planes of his massive pectoral muscles, peppered with a smattering of dark hair leading down his torso and thinning out to a happy trail beneath his navel. His view of his lover's warm skin glistening in the steamy room was a sight to behold.

"Well, now you have me naked. What are you going to do with me?" Nick grinned wolfishly. He was clearly enjoying this little game.

Alex didn't really know what he was doing. He was kind of winging it. He knew what his end game was, but how he was going to get there, he hadn't thought through. The only thing he was sure of was that he was enjoying taking control. Perhaps the events of today had inspired him to be a bit more bolder than usual. Besides, undressing his man had been fun, and slipping into the hot sudsy water with him was going to be wonderful.

"Maybe, you could take my clothes off? If you want?" Alex said bashfully.

Why am I so shy? I've been naked with him before!

"Oh, it would be my pleasure!" Nick smiled wickedly as he swooped in and began slowly shucking Alex's clothes. Soon they were both naked and the tub was almost full, the air thick with steam and the flowery scent of the bath oil.

"What now?" Nick asked, his cock getting harder by the moment.

"Now, we relax in the tub. You can get in first."

Nick complied, stepping into the large round tub and sitting down, getting himself comfortable. Alex then joined him, positioning himself in front of Nick, gently laying back on his lover's muscular chest. Alex reached over and pushed the button to activate the spa jets. It always surprised Alex how quiet the huge spa bath was when switched on, the powerful motor only emitting a low, strangely relaxing hum. The water began bubbling, the surface quickly blanketing itself in a thick fragrant layer of white suds. Alex closed his eyes and let the heat from the water and his lover's body seep into every muscle.

"Touch me." he whispered, and Nick's hands began slowly exploring Alex's body. He ran them over his belly, up his sides and across his chest. He started to lay gentle, featherlight touches to Alex's nipples, circling them and occasionally plucking them with his thumbs. They quickly started to harden and Nick continued to stimulate the sensitive nubs while gently kissing and nibbling his neck.

Alex moaned in appreciation, running his own hands up and down Nick's huge tree trunk thighs. Nick tilted his head slightly and began working his lips on Alex's shoulder, while his hands slowly moved down to Alex's cock and balls. He slowly pumped Alex with one hand while massaging his balls with the other. The multiple sensations coalesced, setting his nerves aflame. He could feel his orgasm approaching.

"Stop."

Nick immediately stilled his hands, "Are you okay?" he whispered in Alex's ear, sounding concerned.

"Oh, yes, it's just... I don't want to... not yet."

"Did you want me to do something else instead?"

Alex knew what he wanted. He hadn't been comfortable asking before now. But over the last few days, he had come to adore Nick and trusted him completely. He knew that Nick was the one. He shifted so he could see Nick's face.

"Will you... make love to me?"

"Are you sure? I don't want to push you into..."

"I'm sure. You're not. I want to. I want you to be my first. I want to feel you inside me. Please, will you make love to me?"

Nick had initially looked concerned, but his features quickly softened into an expression of deep yearning and love.

"It would be my honour, Alex. Come on, let's get dried off and we'll move this into the bedroom."

Alex pulled the bath plug, carefully rose, then stepped out of the huge tub. He grabbed a couple of big fluffy towels and passed one to Nick. They quickly towelled off then stepped into the bedroom. Alex pulled back the covers, then lay on the bed with Nick joining him.

"How do you want me?" Alex's voice was shaky with nerves.

"With your back, you'll be more comfortable on your side with me spooning you from behind."

Alex shifted into position and Nick moved in behind him to hold him in his strong arms, kissing the back of his neck and shoulders. Alex shivered in response.

"If at anytime you want to stop, just say so. I won't be angry." Nick said, his voice soft but serious.

"Thank you, but I trust you. I know you won't hurt me."

"It might hurt a little at first, but I promise it will turn into pleasure very quickly. But regardless, we can stop at any time. All you have to do is say the word."

Alex turned his head and kissed Nick, then leaned over and grabbed the lube and condoms from the bedside table, and handed them to his lover.

Nick gently motioned for Alex to lay back down and he began laying down gentle kisses, starting at his neck and working his way down his spine. Alex's cock was already hard as granite, but Nick's attentions were making him harder still. He bit his lower lip as he moaned with pleasure.

Nick opened the lid of the lube and squeezed a small amount onto his fingers. He gently lifted one of Alex's legs forward to give him better access, then carefully swirled the cool gel around Alex's puckered opening.

"I need to prepare you first, open you up so I'll fit inside you. Just relax and enjoy."

Nick carefully pushed one finger against his opening, then gently pressed it inside, a little at a time, until he was up to the second knuckle. Alex felt full and the stretching sensation burned.

"Just breathe, Alex. Relax and let yourself open up for me," Nick said reassuringly. He withdrew his finger then added more lube. This time he pressed two fingers against his hole, then breached him again. The stretch burned again, but quickly dissipated, as Nick moved his fingers slightly, scissoring and stretching his hole.

Suddenly, Nick brushed against something deep inside, and Alex's central nervous system felt like it had been hit with a bolt of lightening. The feeling was unlike anything he had ever experienced before.

"That's your prostate. You want me to do that again?"

Alex couldn't speak, he just nodded. He gasped as Nick touched the little bundle of nerves again, and Alex started moving his hips involuntarily, trying to fuck himself on Nick's invading fingers.

"Relax, boy! Let me make this good for you."

Alex tried to still himself, but when Nick slid a third finger in, he lost all sense of reason. He moaned and begged and pleaded.

"Please, Sir, please!"

Nick withdrew his fingers and Alex gasped at the sudden empty feeling. He thought he'd done something wrong, but calmed when he turned his head to see Nick rolling on the condom and lubing himself up.

"Are you ready? I'm going to take this nice and slow." Nick said as he pressed his cock against Alex's entrance. He pushed forward slowly, just enough for the head to breach his hole. The sting and stretch was more powerful than what he felt with Nick's fingers.

"Just breathe, Alex. I'll let you get used to it before I go any deeper, I promise. That's it, relax and enjoy."

The sting slowly ebbed away, replaced with a delicious feeling of fullness. Nick pressed forward, past the inner ring of muscles, slowly and carefully until he was fully seated within Alex's passage, his cock nudging against Alex's gland.

Alex had never felt anything like it. Nick's cock was so huge, but somehow he had fit all of it inside. He felt like he was going to come apart at the seams if they didn't start moving soon. Nick pulled back slightly then plunged back in, brushing Alex's prostate again.

"Oh my God! That's so... it's so big!"

"I told you I'd make it good for you. My sweet, sweet boy. Let me make love to you."

"Yes!" Alex replied breathlessly, as Nick began pushing in and out, slowly increasing his pace.

"Fuck, you're so tight! You're amazing, Alex. Let me love on you. Take it all for me, baby."

Nick leaned forward and brought their lips together, changing his angle slightly and increasing his pace again as he repeatedly hit Alex's gland over and over. Kissing at this angle was slightly awkward, but Alex was lost in the moment, moaning into his lover's mouth as the pleasure and passion burned through him.

"I'm not going to last long. You're so tight and you feel so good. I need you to come for me, Alex. Come now!"

Alex's whole body spasmed and, despite not having touched his cock as they made love, Alex came, shot after shot. His orgasm hitting him like a freight train. Alex's inner passage clenched tightly around Nick's cock, and his lover roared through his own orgasm, filling the condom with his load.

Nick held Alex in his arms, kissing his shoulder and murmuring sweet words in his ear. Alex basked in the afterglow of their lovemaking, as their heavy breathing calmed and synchronised.

Just as he was about to tumble into sleep, Alex realised something had changed deep inside him. Not just the loss of his virginity, but something that had crept up a bit at a time. The last shard of ice had crumbled away from his heart. The powerful man that now held him so tightly in his arms had somehow changed everything. Alex realised he could no longer deny the strong, deep emotions that Nick inspired in him.

Alex really was in love with Nick.

Chapter 20

AFTER BREAKFAST, Alex decided that since he was back in his own home, he shouldn't let himself get too far out of his normal routine. It was Monday morning, and he hadn't done much in the way of work over the last few days. He really needed to get some filming done. He had several completed cupcake videos in reserve, ready to be uploaded at anytime, but he always felt more comfortable having a selection of videos ready, just in case he needed to take some time off due to his back injury.

"What are your plans for today?" he asked Nick, who was finishing off his coffee and absently picking at one of the apple and cranberry muffins Alex had baked early that morning. Alex suspected Nick wasn't a fan of apple and/or cranberry, but was eating it anyway, probably because he didn't want to offend.

He's worried about offending me. Maybe he loves me too? Oh don't be ridiculous! He might like *me, but it's too soon for love. I'm just going crazy.*

"Oh, I need to check in with work and get some paperwork done. I brought my laptop, so I won't have to actually go into the office."

"Well, I'm going to do some filming in the kitchen today, so you are welcome to use my home office if you need some peace and quiet to work." Alex said as he gathered the breakfast plates and took them to the sink for washing.

"I'll be happy out here, if that's okay. I'm keen to watch you work, if that won't be too distracting for you?"

Alex smirked, "You're always a distraction, but I'm happy for you to watch. Just keep in mind that I'll be recording audio as well as video, so you'll have to be quiet while I work."

Nick came up behind Alex at the sink as he washed the breakfast dishes, snaking his arms around him, "I'll be as quiet as a mouse," Nick said in a hushed tone, "I just want to see my boy do what he does."

Alex turned in his arms, leaned up and planted a chaste kiss on Nick's inviting lips.

God, this man is amazing. I can't believe how much I love him.

"Don't worry. We can be as loud as we like later." Alex said with a cheeky grin, then returned to the dishes.

Nick chuckled softly, then murmured in his ear that he would be holding Alex to that. Alex shivered with anticipation and at the delightfully naughty images that declaration conjured up.

Nick returned to the living room, pulled out his laptop from his overnight bag and set it up on the coffee table. Alex left him to his work and began setting up the kitchen for filming. He wiped down the bench tops, pulled out all the equipment and ingredients he would need, then began setting up the main camera tripod.

Alex would be making something special, inspired by the erotic bubble bath they had enjoyed the previous evening. The cupcakes themselves would be his standard vanilla bean cake mix, but they would be topped with mounds of soft royal icing and dotted with beautiful little love hearts made from red fondant. The royal icing would set and become thick and solid, holding the love hearts in place.

Nick watched on as Alex turned on the large lighting rig above, adjusted the camera and began work on mixing the cake batter, explaining to the camera what he was doing as he did it.

Once the cupcakes were baked, he left them to cool on the kitchen table while he began rolling out the red fondant and cutting out the heart shapes with a teeny tiny cookie cutter he found several years ago on eBay. Alex then began beating the egg whites, icing sugar and lemon juice in his big stand mixer. The royal icing was impossibly white, like a big bowl of thick liquid marshmallow.

Using a spoon, he piled the thick white topping on to each of the cupcakes, then carefully started placing the love hearts across the surface. Alex set the completed cupcakes on a wire wrack to set, then started cleaning up all the equipment he had used and wiping down the bench tops again. Once this was complete, the icing was set and the cupcakes were ready for displaying so Alex could begin taking still images of his creations.

"All clear, you don't have to be quiet any more. I'm just taking photos now."

Nick started making a series of goofy exaggerated yelling noises, which left them both in stitches. Once they had calmed down, Alex returned to his work. He spent almost an hour taking photos of the gorgeous little cakes, making sure the lighting was just right and changing the angles occasionally, until he was satisfied with the images he had taken. At last, he switched off the overhead lighting rig and turned to see Nick watching him, an awe-struck look on his face.

"What?" Alex said with confusion.

"Wow. That was amazing. I've watched a few of your videos, but I had no idea how much time it takes to actually make them. The effort you put in, the attention to detail. And those cupcakes look stunning. So beautiful. They remind me of our bath last night."

Alex dashed across the room and into Nick's arms. He kissed him deeply and Nick returned the kiss, clutching him to his broad chest.

"What was that for?" Nick said with a puzzled smile.

"You get me. You actually get me. I love that you knew exactly what had inspired me today."

"Of course I get you, Alex. I love you so much."

Alex was stunned by his admission.

Was Nick being serious, or was it just a Freudian slip?

"You do?"

"Oh, I probably shouldn't have said that. It's too soon. We've only known each other for less than a week. But I do, I really do love you. Please don't freak out or anything."

"No, no. I love you too. Oh my God, after last night, I realised that's how I feel too. It crept up on me bit by bit, then suddenly hit me all at once. I know it's happened quickly, but I love you so much."

Nick swooped in and kissed him passionately. The heat and electricity that passed through them was unlike anything they had felt before. Their mutual love, laid bare for all to see, brought them to a new and dizzying level, and their passion was like fire.

Alex broke the kiss and stepped back, grinning like a loon.

This beautiful man loves me. He actually loves me. And I love him. How can this be possible? I never thought this would happen. But I'm so grateful it has.

"Well, as much as I'd like to keep kissing you all day, I really do need to get the rest of my work done. I'm going to be in the home office editing for a few hours." Alex said. He gave Nick a quick chaste kiss, grabbed the cameras off the kitchen table and headed into the home office to get to work.

There really wasn't any urgency in doing the editing immediately, but Alex could tell if he didn't break things up when he did, they would end up spending the day making out and making love. Not that that was such a horrible prospect, but Alex took his business seriously and needed to keep to his schedule where ever possible. While a day of passion and sex would be wonderful, he didn't want to fall into the habit of blowing off work.

Once sat in front of the computer, the rest of the world melted away and Alex focussed exclusively on editing the video he just made. The hours drifted by unnoticed. Once the edited video had finished rendering and was ready to upload to his cloud server, he began working on touching up the still images of the cupcakes. These would be used on social media, video thumbnails and on his website. As he finished, Alex glanced at the clock in the corner of the screen, and realised it was nearly dinnertime. He'd been so distracted by his work, Alex had completely forgotten to take a break for lunch. His stomach was rumbling and, as if on cue, an enticing aroma of tomatoes and garlic wafted in from the direction of the kitchen.

Alex quickly shut down his computer and followed his nose, finding Nick in the kitchen washing up dishes. The oven was on and the smell of lasagna was unmistakable.

"You made dinner? I'm so sorry! I should have done that. You're a guest and I'm being a terrible host. I can't believe I..."

Nick cut him off with a kiss, pressing him backwards until he was backed up against the fridge.

"It's was my pleasure, baby. I wanted to make you dinner. Besides, I'd like to think I'm more than just a guest..." Nick said, then began kissing the sweet spot on Alex's neck.

Alex was still a little floaty from the mind blowing kiss, but now Nick was driving him out of his mind. Alex let out a wanton moan of pleasure.

"Mmm, I love all the little noises I pull from you. So sexy. So beautiful."

The alarm on the oven timer chose that moment to go off, breaking the spell between them. Nick kissed Alex's forehead, then went over to the oven to take out the lasagna.

"I kind of improvised the recipe, since I couldn't find any minced beef in the freezer, so I made a mixed vegetable lasagna instead. I hope that's okay."

"Wow, it looks and smells amazing. You can improvise any time you like." Alex smiled as Nick's face lit up under his praise.

The lasagna had a glorious layer of golden melted cheese on top, bubbling and aromatic. Nick moved gracefully to the fridge and pulled out a beautiful bowl of mixed salad to accompany the meal.

This man is so at home in the kitchen. He makes me dinner. He likes dodgy old movies. He makes me crazy with just a kiss. Could he be any more perfect?

"Why don't you grab us some drinks while I plate this up. The table is already set." Nick said as he started cutting into the cooling lasagna.

Sure enough, the big kitchen table was set with two place mats, cutlery and glasses. He even found the cloth napkins from the bottom kitchen drawer that Alex virtually never used, since it's was usually only himself at the table. Alex grabbed some lemon iced tea from the fridge and poured two glasses. Nick promptly brought over their plates and the two men sat.

"This is amazing. What did you put in it?"

"I just grabbed what I could out of the vegetable drawer. I grated up some carrots, zucchini and sweet potato, then used them to make a tomato, spinach and veggie sauce. I hope it's good."

Alex took a forkful of the lasagna and tasted it. The flavour was extraordinary. Just the right amount of garlic without being overpowering. The sauteed vegetables were flavourful and the sauce was rich and slightly spicy. Alex couldn't contain his moan.

"You need to write down everything you did. This is the most amazing lasagna I've ever tasted. Seriously, I never thought a vegetable lasagna could taste this good!"

Nick positively glowed under his praise. Despite being a successful businessman, Alex got the impression Nick rarely got genuine praise for his efforts, especially away from his work. Alex vowed there and then that his man would always know how appreciated and loved he was.

"Can I ask you a stupid question?" Nick said cautiously.

"Better than anyone I know..."

Nick gasped with mock indignation, "Ha! That was vicious, but I love your comic timing." he chuckled.

"What did you want to know?"

"Well, you seem to make a lot of cupcakes..."

"Kind of an occupational hazard in my line of work. I have to make multiple cupcakes each time I make a video, just in case one doesn't turn out right or I accidentally drop one. What about it?"

"Um, what do you do with them all? I mean, you can't possibly eat all of them?"

Alex laughed, "No, goodness no! I maybe eat one from each batch, just to make sure they taste right. Well, that's the story I'm sticking to. Anyway, the rest I put into disposable plastic containers and put them in the freezer. Then a few times a year, I load them all into the car and anonymously deliver them to soup kitchens, women's refuges, anywhere they might be appreciated."

Nick looked genuinely surprised. Perhaps he figured Alex would just throw them away, a horrible waste of food that Alex could never abide. Maybe he was amused at the thought of Alex leaving the house on clandestine moonlit cupcake deliveries. Alex had to admit, the thought kind of tickled him too.

"You are an amazing man, Alex. I'm so lucky to have found you."

Once they finished dinner and the dishes were washed, they retired to the bedroom where Nick insisted on giving Alex another full body massage. Alex felt a little guilty just lying back and getting all the attention, but it was clear that Nick was really getting off on exploring his body. Alex was still a little shocked that someone as beautiful as Nick would be so turned on by someone like him, but Alex could see the genuine love and devotion in his lover's eyes, and he knew that their attraction was not only mutual but explosive now that they had declared their love for each other.

After the massage, Alex laid Nick down and used the same massage oil to explore his body. Slowly, tentatively, he rubbed every inch of his body. The vast plains of his pectorals; his thick meaty biceps; those powerful thighs that could crush a boulder. He touched and teased everywhere... except one certain place. Nick was writhing with need and his cock was hard as nails. But Alex wanted to try something. Something he had been fantasising about for years.

"Please, baby. Stop teasing me. I need you."

Alex couldn't help but feel a little smug that he had managed to make his man-mountain lover quiver with unabashed need. He shifted position so he was crouched next to Nick, facing away from him. He bent down and slowly licked up his thick shaft, from the fragrant tuft at the base, to the head glistening with precum. Nick groaned incoherently, babbling and begging for more. Alex licked the dewy drop from his crown and the salty tang exploded on his tongue.

"Please!" Nick was damn near insane with need. Alex could tell he was testing his lover's control, and that any moment now, he may just lose it entirely. That one taste of Nick's essence was addictive and, although Alex had no experience giving blow jobs, he'd read enough sexy romance books and seen enough porn to know what would drive his man wild, and he had a feeling he would enjoy it too.

Alex grabbed Nick's shaft with one hand and brought the head to his lips. He lapped his tongue around and around, then sucked it into his mouth. He rubbed the crown against his tongue, feeling Nick's whole body writhe beneath him. He upped the suction and took a little more of the mighty cock into his mouth. Nick was thick and long, so he doubted he would be able to take all of it on his first attempt, but he would try his best. Alex relaxed his throat muscles and pushed forward, stretching his lips and moving further down until Nick's cock grazed the back of his throat. He bobbed back up without gagging and let the cock fall out of his mouth.

"Was that good? Am I doing it right?"

"Oh my God, baby. Yes, that was amazing. You're a natural!"

Alex, bursting with pride at Nick's unrestrained praise, returned to sucking, now confident in his efforts. He used his hand to slowly pump Nick's shaft as he increased the suction on the crown, stopping occasionally to go deep, eliciting growls and moans from his lover. The more Nick growled, the more turned on Alex became. He was no longer ashamed to admit how much he loved the idea of being dominated by Nick. Being on the receiving end of such power and strength was beyond erotic. Which gave him an idea that would be mind blowing for both of them. He let go of Nick's cock and stopped sucking.

"Please don't stop! I'm so close!"

Alex turned to his lover and coyly smiled.

"Sir, would you do something for me?"

Nick sat up, his eyes feral with want, "Anything! Tell me what you need, boy."

"I need you to... fuck my throat, Sir."

Nick was silent for a moment. Alex figured he wasn't expecting to hear those words come from him, but they clearly enflamed his lust. He growled low and was barely containing himself.

"Are you sure? I don't want to hurt you."

"I trust you. I want it. I want you to fuck my throat. Please, Sir."

Nick grabbed Alex by the hair, his fingers tightly holding on to his curls. He carefully pulled Alex up to his face and kissed him roughly.

"If you want me to stop, pinch my thigh and I'll stop immediately. You understand?"

"Yes, Sir."

"You're such a good boy. I love you so much."

And with that, Nick thrust Alex's head down onto his cock. He willingly opened his mouth, relaxed his throat, and let Nick have control, thrusting in and out of his moist heat. He would stop now and again to allow Alex to take a breath, but his cock never left Alex's mouth. Alex had never been so turned on, and the sound of Nick growling as he thrust upwards, fucking his face, was enough to make him come harder than ever before, and all without even touching himself.

"I'm gonna come. If you don't want it in your throat, pinch me now!"

Alex wasn't going to stop now. He wanted this. He needed this. The slide of Nick's shaft along his tongue as he pressed Alex's head down as far as he could was delicious. The thick meat in his mouth spasmed and flooded him with hot spurts of come. Alex swallowed again and again, trying not to lose a single precious drop. Nick was panting as his orgasm ripped through him.

Eventually, Nick released him and gently guided Alex up to face him, pressing their lips together.

"Mmm, I can taste myself on you. That was... wow! I can't believe we just did that. Who knew you were such a dirty boy!"

"I guess you inspired me. That was the most incredible thing ever. I don't know how we'll top that."

"Sounds like a challenge to me." Nick chuckled, then kissed Alex on the forehead. The melted into each other's arms and quickly fell asleep.

Chapter 21

NICK WOKE up early, just as the sun was rising. Alex was still sound asleep beside him, thoroughly exhausted from their night of lovemaking. Nick couldn't stifle his grin. He had never been happier in his entire life.

After so many years of searching, he had finally found the other half of his soul. A man who so perfectly complimented him in every possible way. His boy was sweet, generous, loving and funny as hell. The fact that they were so compatible in the bedroom was just icing on the cake. Or cupcake in this case.

Once this business with Jack was dealt with, something Nick hoped would happen sooner rather than later, he wanted to help Alex to rebuild his life. The poor guy had been living in darkness for so long, it would take a lot of time and support to acclimatise him to a life that didn't depend on security systems and hiding away from the world. Nick was only too happy to be his guide, and was set on standing by Alex for as long as it took.

Nick still found it incomprehensible how Alex had managed to cope with his prolonged isolation. He had no family or friends. He rarely had face-to-face contact with other people. It's a wonder his boy didn't go stark raving mad from loneliness. Nick wanted to bring Alex back into the light, get him used to being around other people again.

But this would no doubt be a slow and gradual process. Nick was friends with a highly regarded therapist, and he hoped he would be able to convince Alex to speak with him. Joshua Maddox had helped Nick with his own issues over the years, and he was certain Alex would benefit from his advice.

Deciding to let Alex sleep in, Nick carefully got out of bed and showered. Once dressed, he headed out to the kitchen and made two cups of steaming coffee. One for himself and one for Russell, the security guard who had been standing guard outside all night.

He brought the mug of coffee to the grateful guard, who reported nothing unusual happening at Nick's house, nor any suspicious activity here during the night.

"My replacement will be here soon. I'll brief him on everything when he gets here, then head home. I'll be back tonight."

"Thanks, Russell. We appreciate all your hard work."

Nick returned inside and sat at the kitchen table. He checked his email on his phone as he sipped his coffee. He had a message from Andrew reporting that everything was running smoothly at the office, but he needed Nick to sign some contracts to get the security installations arranged. Andrew said he would be dropping by Alex's house on his way to work with the papers that needed signing.

Nick texted Russell to let him know his assistant would be arriving shortly and to grant him access, then set about preparing some breakfast for him and Alex. As he was gathering ingredients out of the fridge, Nick heard movement coming from the bedroom, followed by the sound of the shower.

Perfect timing!

Nick got to work, and by the time Alex emerged from the bedroom, looking refreshed and ready for the day ahead, he was plating up two big servings of scrambled eggs and toast.

"Good morning, babe"

"Good morning to you too. You know, if you keep cooking for me like this, I'm gonna get very spoiled," Alex said with a grin.

"Excellent! I love spoiling you," Nick replied, handing Alex a freshly made cup of coffee. The two men sat down at the kitchen table and tucked into their breakfast.

As they sat and ate, Nick couldn't help noticing how quickly and easily he had slipped into domestic bliss. Okay, the circumstance that had forced Alex and Nick into living together temporarily were certainly out of the ordinary, but something about it felt right. Natural. The simple pleasures of cooking a meal for his lover; standing side by side as they washed the dishes; holding each other as they slept. All of it felt like it was meant to be.

All of this was new territory for Nick. But it sparked his imagination. What would it be like to live with Alex full time? Would they continue to enjoy their newly found domesticity? Would they travel together and explore exotic, far flung destinations? Would they eventually get married? All these ideas buzzed in his mind, probably because, for the first time in his life, Nick felt these were actual, real possibilities. Not just some hypothetical, abstract ideas that *may* happen with *some* person he hadn't met yet at *some* point in the future.

Nick snapped back into reality. What was happening here and now was more important for the moment. He could dream about the future once the threat to Alex had been neutralised.

"Are you planning on doing more filming today?"

"No, not today. But I do have a conference call with my book publishers this morning. I'm currently working on my latest cookbook, and they want to go over everything and make sure I'm still on schedule."

"When do you have to start your call?" Nick enquired as he finished his plate of eggs.

Alex looked at a battered old cuckoo clock on the kitchen wall, which Nick thought looked totally out of place in the otherwise modern kitchen, "In about ten minutes. I'll be in the home office, but I'll probably be a couple of hours. My book editor is a real chatterbox, and once she gets started..."

Nick chuckled. He had a few people in his office who were just like that. He gathered up their empty plates and took them to the sink.

"Do you want another coffee before you start your call?"

"Oh, yes please. I'll need it if I'm going to get through this meeting. I must have written at least ten cookbooks with this publisher, but they act like I have no idea what I'm doing. They micromanage everything.

Don't be shocked if I come out of the office with clumps of hair torn out!" Alex laughed.

Nick set about making another coffee for Alex. He chuckled at the look of frustration on his boy's face. Nick quickly realised that Alex hated the fact that his new coffee machine would rarely cooperate with him, but would work every time without fuss for Nick. Alex seemed to genuinely believe the 'devil machine,' as he frequently referred to it, was deliberately misbehaving.

Nick gave him a quick chaste kiss, handed over the mug of steaming coffee and watched as his boy disappeared into the home office, closing the door behind him.

Despite Alex only being in the next room, Nick keenly felt his absence immediately.

This is getting ridiculous. Get a grip!

Nick distracted himself by washing up the dishes and cleaning up the kitchen. As he was finishing, he heard muffled voices coming from outside.

Ah, the security guards must be doing their shift change over.

He put the washed and dried dishes away, then withdrew to the living room to retrieve his laptop. He had a few reports from the marketing department he wanted to review this morning, and set himself up on the couch.

A few minutes later, there was a knock on the front door. Nick stood, walked over to the entry way and opened the front door. Standing on the front porch was Andrew, clutching a file folder.

"Good morning, Andrew. Do you have time for a coffee?"

"Oh, I have all the time in the world," Andrew said, handing over the folder.

Nick turned around and allowed Andrew to come in. He opened the folder, but discovered it was filled with blank paper. Nick thought this was highly unusual. Andrew never made mistakes like this.

"I think you brought the wrong file..."

Nick was cut off by a sharp pain in his neck. His vision started to blur and his legs became weak. As he collapsed to the floor of the entry way, and through increasingly fuzzy vision, Nick saw two things that alarmed him. Russell laying face down on the outside porch, and Andrew looming over Nick, holding a syringe.

As the darkness quickly claimed him, Nick's last thoughts were of Alex. How much he loved him. How much he needed him. But above all else, how he'd failed to protect him.

Chapter 22

AFTER JUST over two hours of endless conversation on the group video chat with the team from his book publisher, Alex's patience was officially exhausted. He wasn't the most social person at the best of times, but with the stress of everything that had happened over the last few days, coupled with being forced to endure a meeting that was, more or less, exactly the same as the meeting from last month, he was ready to end this call and get on with his day with Nick.

Alex wrapped up the call, shut down the laptop and headed out to the kitchen in search of Nick and more coffee. However, Nick was nowhere to be found. He wasn't in the kitchen or the living room. He wasn't in the bedroom or bathroom either.

Maybe he needed to go to the office with his assistant, and didn't want to disturb me?

Alex returned to the kitchen and found the breakfast dishes washed up and put away. The counter tops had been wiped down and everything was as neat and tidy as it usually was. Alex placed his empty coffee mug by the devil coffee machine, intent on refilling it with more precious caffeinated goodness.

He smiled and thought to himself how kind, generous and loving Nick was. He was never selfish, nor did he demand things from Alex that he wouldn't be prepared to do himself. The simple act of making breakfast and letting Alex sleep in spoke volumes about the kind of man his lover truly was. Come what may, he would never allow anything to come between them. Although their relationship was relatively new, it was the most precious thing in Alex's life, and not even Jack and the serious threat he posed was going to spoil their burgeoning love.

Alex flicked on the coffee machine and started to make himself a really strong cup of coffee. As the liquid dispensed into the mug, Alex pulled his phone out of his pocket and called Nick. He wanted to know what was happening and when to expect him back. Alex was thinking of ordering in pizza for dinner. He had never had meals delivered to the house before, but with all the extra security, plus the fact that Jack already knew where he lived, Alex's rules seemed pretty redundant now.

Within moments, the faint sound of a phone ringing came from somewhere outside the front door. Alex thought that was strange.

Perhaps Nick had dropped his phone on the way out?

Alex moved towards the front door, but when he tried to open it, it wouldn't budge. Someone had apparently dead bolted the door from the inside. Alex looked to the bowl on the entry table where he kept his house keys, only to find the keys were missing.

Did Nick take them with him? No, the door is locked from the inside. What the hell is going on?

Alex looked out the front window and recoiled in horror. In the middle of the courtyard, the bodies of Russell and Nick lay face down. On each of their backs was a single red rose.

OH MY GOD.

Jack is here. He's locked me in with him.

Alex didn't have time to process what had happened outside. He couldn't tell if the men were dead or just unconscious. He lurched over to the security panel and hit the panic button. When he first moved into the house, Alex had insisted on having several panic buttons hidden around the house, each triggering the silent alarm and alerting the back-to-base monitoring company that something was wrong.

"That won't do you any good. I disconnected the phone line. The alarm system is deactivated."

A chill ran down Alex's spine as he slowly turned in the direction of the cold, familiar voice. Standing at the far end of the living room was Jack. He was holding a large bunch of red roses and grinning. The smile didn't reach his eyes. The same creepy expression he wore just moments before he began stabbing Alex all those years ago.

"What did you do to them, Jack? Are they dead?" Alex was afraid of the answer.

"They got in my way. And you know how I feel about people getting between us..."

Alex's blood ran cold. Nick was dead. His world was crumbling around him. After so many years of loneliness, he had finally found someone who loved him. Now, the love of his life had been cruelly snatched from him. He couldn't breathe. He wanted to sob. But he was numb. Alex knew in that moment he would never love again, and that he was most likely about to die.

Jack slowly moved forward, holding up the bouquet of flowers, offering them to Alex, "I brought these for you. You always loved roses. I sent you so many when we were dating."

"We had one date, Jack, and it was awful. You're insane. You need help."

"What I need is for you to stop with this 'playing hard to get' routine. It's getting old. Do you have any idea how hard I've worked to find you?" Jack continued to slowly approach.

"Do you have any idea how far I travelled. I spent two years searching Perth for you without luck. Eventually, I figured you lied to me in your love letter you left for me on your door. Another little game to keep me interested. I didn't know what to do. After Perth, I couldn't go back to Cooper's Landing. So I went to Melbourne and started a new life, hoping that fate would drop you back into my arms. Then one day, it did. You jumped into the back of my boss's car and directed me right to your house!"

Alex could taste bile in the back of his throat. After all his rules. After how careful he had been. It had all been for nothing. He himself had been the one to lead Jack straight to his home. Alex couldn't believe it. He shook his head, wishing it wasn't true. Alex's own actions had lead the love of his life to his death, and he had no one to blame but himself.

I should have stuck to my rules. I shouldn't have left the house. My own greed killed Nick.

"We are meant to be, sweetheart. The universe wants us to be together. You can't deny it."

"NO! *Nick and I* were meant to be. But you destroyed it, like you destroy everything. You're a crazy, selfish bastard and I hate you! I will never love you. I could *never* love you." Alex spat out, his words laced with venomous hatred.

"Do you think that big oaf out there loved you? He could never have loved you like I do. He was so stupid. He didn't even check my references when he hired me. I can give you more than he ever could."

"I don't want it. You robbed me of my life, Jack. You robbed me of the best years of my life. You robbed me of my one true love. Now, I have nothing left to live for. Now, I have nothing left to lose..." Alex carefully backed himself toward the entry table and reached gently for the bowl.

Jack's features contorted from creepy smile to outright fury. His face went red and his eyes burned with hatred.

"You're the selfish one! After everything I did for you! You don't deserve love. You don't deserve anything!" he shrieked as he lunged forward, dropping the roses and brandishing a syringe.

Alex swung the heavy ceramic bowl and it smashed against Jack's head, knocking him backwards and momentarily stunning him. Alex seized his chance and made a dash for the kitchen. Jack roared in fury and lumbered unsteadily after him, blood pouring down his face.

Alex grabbed random objects off the kitchen counters and hurled them at Jack. The toaster, a canister of sugar, a chopping board, most of which bounced ineffectually off his outstretched arms. Alex wielded his walking cane like a sword. He swung it as hard as he could, striking Jack in the shoulder. The force was enough to splinter the cane and it fell to the floor.

Alex was running out of weapons. But Alex spotted the bastard coffee machine, solid and heavy and capable of inflicting some serious damage. Alex wrenched it up off the counter, not caring it was still plugged in, and threw it toward Jack. The power cable snapped as it hit Jack square in the chest, knocking the wind out of him. Alex grabbed a large knife from the knife block at the far end of the kitchen counter, acutely aware he had backed himself into a corner, and held it up in front of him.

"Get the fuck away from me, Jack. I won't warn you again. Stay back!" he shouted.

Jack's eyes filled with pure rage. He held up the syringe and lurched forward. Alex thrust the knife, slicing Jack's forearm. Jack lunged again, but missed Alex entirely. Alex barrelled forward and swung the knife blindly, hoping to strike something painful. It plunging deep into Jack's right inner thigh. Jack howled in agony.

The ensuing horror of screaming and wild spurts of blood distracted Alex momentarily, giving Jack the brief opportunity to thrust the syringe into Alex's arm before he could pull away. Jack stumbled back, gripping the massive leg wound, backing into the fridge and slumping to the floor. Blood ran freely between his fingers and he appeared to lose consciousness.

Alex staggered backwards, his vision blurry. He stumbled into the kitchen table, dropping the knife. As he fell to the floor, his head hit one of the chairs with a sickening thud. Alex lay of the ground, his face mashed against the cool slate tiles. The room was spinning, and Alex couldn't concentrate on what was happening. The world grew dark and Alex couldn't prevent his tumble into oblivion.

Chapter 23

NICK AWOKE to someone shaking him violently. His head was fuzzy and his eyelids felt heavy. He couldn't move, like his limbs were weighed down. He heard a voice that sounded muffled and far away.

"Are you okay? Mr Hawke? Wake up!"

Nick shook his head and struggled to open his eyes. He was lying on concrete. He rolled over and was blinded by the bright sun above.

The courtyard. What happened? Why am I on the ground?

He looked around and saw the source of the voice. Russell was crouched next to him. He had a graze on his face and his eyes looked unfocused.

"Are you okay, sir?"

"I think so. What the hell happened?"

"Your assistant. He took me by surprise and drugged me with a syringe. Next thing I know, I was waking up next to you on the ground."

My assistant? Andrew! He had a syringe.

ALEX!

Nick tried to sit up. His body was still suffering from the effects of the tranquilliser. He struggled to get up and headed for the front door. When he found it was locked, Nick began banging on it wildly, praying he wasn't too late. He didn't know how long he had been unconscious, but he knew if Andrew was inside the house, and that Andrew was capable of overpowering two very strong men without much effort, it wouldn't take much for him to overpower and hurt Alex. The thought of Alex hurt filled him with cold dread.

"Alex! Alex, open the door. Can you hear me?"

The silence from the house was deafening. Something terrible had happened. Nick was starting to panic. His mind filled with disturbing images of Alex fighting for his life; of him being restrained and beaten; of him succumbing to his injuries. Nick knew he had to get to Alex, and there wasn't a moment to lose.

"Give me your keys!"

Russell patted his pockets, but found nothing. Andrew clearly didn't want them getting in, and he wasn't taking any chances.

Nick began ramming the door with his shoulder, desperate to break it down. He started kicking the door near the lock and after a few sturdy blows, the wooden door yielded and smashed open, the wooden door jam splintering. Nick surged forward to find the living room resembling a disaster area. Furniture upturned and broken furnishings strewn across the floor. He headed to the kitchen and stumbled back in shock.

The scene before him was horrifying. The kitchen floor was coated in blood. Andrew lay slumped against the fridge door, his face pale and lifeless. Beside him lay a syringe. A heavy pool of blood surrounded his corpse, and spread across the entire floor.

By the kitchen table, Alex lay face down on the blood soaked floor, a knife by his side. The hair on the back of his head was matted with blood. His clothes were soaked in yet more blood. Nick couldn't tell if the blood was from Andrew or Alex. But Alex wasn't moving. He rushed to his boy's side.

"Oh, Jesus. No!"

My Alex. My sweet, beautiful Alex. Please God, No.

"Call an ambulance! And get the police too. Hurry!" Nick bellowed to Russell. He dropped to his knees by Alex. He turned Alex over and checked for a pulse. It was there, but weak; his breathing shallow.

Nick clutched Alex to him closely, desperate to hold him. His eyes pricked with tears as his lover lay limp and lifeless in his arms.

"Don't do this, Alex. Please don't leave me. I spent my life looking for you. You can't go now. Just hold on. Help is on the way."

Nick's head was still fuzzy, and he was finding it hard to stay awake. He fought against the seductive embrace of sleep as he became vaguely aware of sirens outside.

A few moments later, paramedics burst into the house. They lifted Alex out of Nick's arms and they began checking his vitals.

"I think he's been drugged. The syringe is on the floor over there. Is he going to be okay?"

"He has a serious head wound, we need to get him in the ambulance now. You too sir, you need to be checked out as well." one of the paramedics said as he and his partner eased Alex onto a gurney.

"Anything, just help him. Please, he's all I have."

"We'll do everything we can. Can you walk?"

"Yeah, I think so. But I've been drugged too."

Nick staggered out to the street, staying by Alex's side as he was loaded into the back of the ambulance. He saw Detective Kincaid pull up behind the ambulance, but didn't have time to talk to him, the paramedics forcing him and Russell into the back with Alex.

As the ambulance moved off, Nick couldn't hold on any longer and he slumped unconscious on the bench. The last thing he heard was the paramedics trying to get Alex to respond.

Chapter 24

ALEX AWOKE in darkness. The room was cold and the air smelled like antiseptic. His head was throbbing and he felt very dizzy. As his eyes adjusted to the dark, he was finally able to focus. He was lying in a hospital room. No light came from the large window to his right.

It must be the middle of the night.

In the corner of the room, a familiar figure was slumped in a chair.

"Nick," Alex tried to say, but his throat was dry and sore. He could barely manage a whispered croak.

Nick looked like hell. He was unshaven and had dark circles under his eyes. Despite being asleep, he did not look remotely rested.

Alex found a call button by his right hand. He pressed it, hoping someone would come quickly. He desperately needed a drink.

Nick.

He's alive!

Oh my God, I can't believe it!

Moments later, a nurse entered the room and turned on the bedside lamp. Alex winced at the brightness. The nurse was short in stature, with bright red hair and a friendly face. She smiled at Alex.

"Mr Michaels, you're awake. How are you feeling?"

"My head hurts," he croaked, "and I need water."

"I'll bring you something in a moment. I'm just going to check your vitals. Do you want me to wake him?" She said, glancing towards Nick.

"Let him sleep, he looks like he needs it."

"He does. That man hasn't left your side for more than a bathroom break in over four days."

Four days? Had it really been that long?

Once the nurse had finished poking and prodding him, she quietly slipped from the room, returning moments later with a cup of ice chips.

As the tiny shards of ice melted on his tongue and slipped down his throat, the relief was exquisite. Soon his mouth felt better and his throat less hoarse. As he was taking another small mouthful of ice chips, Nick jerked awake. He looked around, dazed for a moment, then focused straight on Alex. He leaped out of the chair and dashed to his side.

"Baby, you're awake! Are you okay?" his features drawn with concern.

"I think so," Alex softly whispered, "My head hurts and my back is throbbing, but otherwise I'm fine. Are you okay? I thought you were dead."

"I'm fine now that I know you're okay," Nick's voice became small, "I was so scared. When I found you, I thought…" his voice broke and he couldn't finish that thought.

"Hey, I'm going to be fine. But you look like crap. You need to get some rest."

"I'm not going anywhere. I'm staying right here with you." Nick said with stubborn authority.

"Well, Mr Michaels needs his rest. The doctor will be here in a few hours to check him over. Now would be a good time for you to go get some rest," the nurse suggested gently, "and perhaps… a shower and a change of clothes?" The nurse smiled sweetly then quickly left the room, no doubt wanting to evacuate the area after that less than subtle bombshell.

Nick looked down at his wrinkled shirt, "Do I really look that bad?" he said, sniffing his shirt and balking, "Okay, maybe she's right."

Alex stifled a chuckle, not confident his throat would take kindly to an attack of the giggles. Nick scowled at him, but Alex knew there was no heat behind it.

"She's right. I'm still really tired. You should go get some rest. I'm only going to be sleeping anyway. Look after yourself for a while, then you can come back and look after me."

"I promise, I'll be back in an hour. Two hours, tops."

"Take your time. I'm not going anywhere. Now give me a kiss and go."

Nick leaned in and gently kissed Alex. He brushed his cheek with his thumb, "I love you, Alex."

"I love you too. See you when I wake up."

Alex closed his eyes as Nick turned and left the room. He fell asleep within seconds.

When Alex woke up, it was midmorning. Nick wasn't back yet. The nurse returned to bring him some breakfast. Mostly mushy porridge and some apple juice. It tasted awful, but it was easy to swallow, which made it the best meal he could possibly hope for.

The doctor made an appearance shortly after breakfast, and explained Alex had been put into an induced coma after sustaining a head injury during the attack. Apparently, Alex's brain had begun swelling and the induced coma helped to bring things back to normal. Alex didn't really understand it all, he was more focused on when he could go home. The doctor insisted on one more night in hospital, just for observation. Alex grumbled, but agreed to stay and rest up. Besides, he didn't really feel up to staging a prison break.

When the doctor left, he had another visitor. Detective Kincaid came to update him on everything and to take his statement. The sight of the big, burly police officer seemed to bring his memories of the attack into clear focus. Up until this point, it had all been a bit fuzzy, but now they were clear as day.

"Mr Michaels, how are you feeling? Are you up for a few questions?"

"Yes, please take a seat."

The detective dragged the chair over from the corner and sat down next to Alex. He pulled out his notebook and pen, then turned to a blank page.

"So, can you tell me, in your own words, what you remember of the incident at your house?"

Alex detailed everything that happened, from waking up and sharing breakfast with Nick, to coming out of the office and being confronted by Jack.

"Nobody has told me, is Jack really dead?"

"Yes, he bled out at the scene."

Alex let out a breath and felt a wave of relief wash over him. Then he froze.

Am I a bad person to feel that way? I took someone's life. Should I feel relieved over killing someone? Will I be arrested?

"Are you going to charge me with murder?" Alex said, his voice barely a whisper.

"No, Mr Michaels. I think it's safe to say you acted in self defence. We won't be laying any charges. But I do have some more questions for you."

"Of course. Anything you need." Alex was just glad he wasn't going to spend the rest of his life in prison. Slightly ironic since he had been living in a prison of his own making for years.

"We managed to identify Jack from fingerprints and dental records. His real name is Adrian Jackson. Does that name mean anything to you?"

Alex tried to think. It didn't seem familiar, "No, I don't think so..."

"How about Conrad Jackson?"

Alex froze.

"The drunk driver who killed my parents?"

"Yes. It seems Adrian was Conrad's younger brother."

You've got to be kidding? Jack's brother killed my parents?

"We haven't got the full picture yet, but it seems Adrian became obsessed with you after the two of you met briefly at the coronial inquest into your parent's deaths."

"I don't remember meeting him. But it was so long ago. I really met him at the inquest?"

"Chances are you never directly interacted with him. He probably saw you there and became fixated. From what I've been able to put together, Adrian had a long history of mental problems. When his parents died in a house fire, his older brother became his legal guardian. When Conrad died, Adrian was left with no one. I believe he became obsessed with you after the inquest, and his obsession grew. Like many stalkers, he built up an elaborate fantasy in his own mind in which the two of you were in love. So when you rejected him, he suffered a severe mental breakdown and lashed out at you."

Alex couldn't believe what he was hearing. He had always wondered why Jack was so fixated on him. The idea that his parent's deaths were indirectly connected to Jack was something he had never considered in his wildest dreams.

"After your attack in Cooper's Landing, I have little information on Adrian's movements. He started using the alias Andrew Charles in Melbourne about four years ago, but how he found you after so many years is still to be determined."

Alex told the detective everything Jack said about going to Perth, then the coincidence of him just happening to get into the back of Nick's car when Jack was driving.

"Wow, what are the odds, huh?" Kincaid said, shaking his head.

"So, what now?"

"I'll right up my reports. The coroner will do his own report. Then it will all be over. All you need to do is sign a statement when you are feeling up to it, then focus on getting well again."

Suddenly, Nick strode into the room looking fresh and rested. He was clean shaven and wearing jeans and a tight black t shirt. Alex thought he looked better than ever.

"Baby, are you feeling better this morning?"

Alex grinned, "Much better. The doctor will let me go home tomorrow. Detective Kincaid just finished filling me in on everything I missed."

The detective rose from his chair, shook Nick's hand and then Alex's. He put away his notebook and made way for Nick to sit down.

"I have everything I need for now. I'll bring the statement for you to sign later today, then I can be out of your hair."

"Thank you for everything, Detective," Nick smiled and took Alex's hand, giving it a gentle squeeze.

The detective nodded stiffly, then left the room.

"You're looking well rested. Wish I could say the same. I've been unconscious for four days, yet I feel like I haven't slept for a month."

Nick kissed the back of Alex's hand, then gently brushed his fingers through his hair.

"Then just lie back and relax. You get some sleep, and I'll be here when you wake up."

Alex was going to argue. He wanted to spend some time with Nick, but his eyes felt heavy and he just couldn't stay awake. He quickly fell asleep as Nick held his hand.

Epilogue

Six Months Later...

AFTER A long day of last minute changes and edits to his latest cookbook, the manuscript was sent through to the publishers and all the photography was complete. Alex was glad to be finally done with it, as it had taken so long to get back into the swing of things after the incident with Jack.

Kelly, his personal assistant, knocked on his office door and asked if he needed anything before she left for the weekend. Alex was ready to put an end to the working week himself, and told Kelly he would see her on Monday.

Collecting his things, Alex headed out of his office and walked toward the lifts. Even after all these months, he still wasn't used to working in Nick's building.

Alex, wanting to create a separation between his work and home life, relocated his business to the ninth floor. The former location of Corona Industries *mysteriously* became available after Alex had mentioned in passing how badly they had treated him on the day he and Nick had first met. Nick never explained the exact circumstances as to why Corona Industries' lease agreement was so suddenly terminated, but given that Nick was the owner of the building, it wasn't difficult to figure out.

The ninth floor was completely renovated to accommodate CupcakeBoy Productions. Part of the floor was soundproofed and converted into a filming studio with a fully functional kitchen set for making his videos. Despite there being no further need for anonymity, Alex continued to not show his face in his videos. Partly to maintain the mystique around his online persona, and partly because he wanted his cupcakes to be the stars of the show, not him.

The rest of the office space included a section for working on his cookbooks, meeting and conference rooms and a small nook for his team of social media managers. Expanding the business and hiring staff to help lift the burden of running the whole operation single-handedly had done wonders for Alex's stress. Plus he had more free time to devote to his relationship with Nick. The changes to the business had quickly made a huge difference both personally and financially. Alex could now focus on video making and cookbooks, and the business was more profitable than ever before.

After Jack's death, Alex didn't return to his little home on the laneway. He simply didn't feel safe there any more. Nick arranged a moving company to pack up his belongings and insisted on Alex moving in with him. Initially, Alex had been resistant to moving in after such a short period of time. But after the first week, living with Nick felt as natural as breathing. Alex had considered selling his house, but decided to keep it for the moment. He hired a contractor and had the house renovated into a more conventional home. The big, imposing walls around the house were demolished, replaced with more conventional fencing, and the courtyard was converted into a tidy little garden. It didn't take long to find a tenant, and now the laneway house was an investment property garnering Alex a steady rental income.

Alex got into the lift and made his way up to Nick's floor. When he stepped out, he was greeted by Lara, Nick's new assistant.

"He's waiting for you in the conference room, Mr Michaels."

"Thanks, Lara."

It had taken Nick several months to find an assistant to replace Andrew/Jack. Initially he refused to hire one. It still stung him that someone who Nick considered to be a friend, actually turned out to be a dangerous psychopath. The whole affair had made Nick question his judgement and his hiring procedures.

But the nature of his work meant he needed help with running the day to day operations of his business, so Nick's HR manager worked tirelessly to find suitable candidates. Eventually, Lara was hired, and Alex loved her. She was efficient, intuitive, and in no way intimidated by Nick. She worked hard and wouldn't take any crap from Nick. Nick still occasionally grumbled about how he missed the days when 'he was the boss' but deep down, Alex knew Nick adored Lara. The woman was amazing.

When he stepped into the conference room, he found Nick sitting at the head of the long meeting table, surrounded by paperwork and file folders.

"Hi, Honey! Sorry I'm late. Traffic was hell."

Nick had the good grace to chuckle at what was now a running joke between them. He stood and took Alex in his arms, kissing him deeply.

"How was your day, babe. Did you end up finishing the book?"

"Yes, finally. All the changes are done and the manuscript is submitted. Printing should begin next month for an August release."

"That's fantastic. Congratulations! Hey, we should go out and celebrate." Nick said, hugging him again.

"How about that nice little Thai place we found in North Fitzroy. I'd love to try that weird mango dessert thing again. I'm still trying to figure out what's in it."

"Anything you want," Nick grinned, "But the chef isn't going to tell you his secret, no matter how many times you beg him!"

"I'm wearing him down..." Alex grumbled.

Nick laughed and Alex scowled at him, which only made Nick laugh more.

"Before we head out to dinner, there's something I wanted to talk to you about, but I didn't want to bring it up until you finished with the book."

Was something wrong? Had something happened?

"Relax. It's nothing bad. I've had an idea for a joint business venture, and I wanted to get your input."

Alex was curious. What kind of joint business venture could a gym mogul and a cupcake guy possibly have?

"I was wondering if you would be interested in writing a cookbook that would be exclusive to my gyms. My idea is 'Healthy Cupcakes for Active People' - what do you think?"

Alex looked at him blankly.

"Well?"

"Healthy cupcakes?"

"Yeah."

"Me making healthy cupcakes?"

"Yeah!"

"Why don't you just cut my heart out? It would hurt less!"

"I'm serious!"

"Healthy cupcakes suck! Everybody knows that."

"Of course they suck! That's why I want you to work your magic."

"I'll find my magic wand..."

"Come on! Over the last six months, I've learned what an incredible cook you are. You are the most talented baker I've ever met. I know if you put your mind to it, you'd be able to come up with a selection of healthy cupcake recipes that not only taste great, but would be good for you too."

Alex had to admit, it would be a challenge.

"So how would this business venture work?"

"Well, I would fund your research. You could work in your own time, bring in nutritionists and any other experts to help you. You'd come up with the recipes. Then put them together in a cookbook like you normally would. We sell the book at my gyms and split the profits."

"If you're funding the research and development, wouldn't selling the books only at your gyms seriously reduce profits? How will you make your money back?"

Nick smiled smugly. Apparently he had been anticipating this question.

"The book would only be exclusive to Hawke's Gym for the first six months. You have a massive online following that will be desperate to get their hands on your new cookbook. They'll come into my gyms to get it and..."

"Some of them might sign up as new members. Well, what happens after six months?"

"We release the book worldwide as normal. Split the book sales. So, what do you say? Wanna be my business partner?" Nick smiled, and flashed his best puppy dog eyes at him.

Alex had to admit, the idea had potential. Both businesses could make a lot of money out of this if they can come up with enough decent recipes. Plus, Alex liked the idea of becoming the first person in history to make a healthy cupcake that didn't taste like garbage.

"It's sounds like fun."

Nick leaped out of his chair and dragged Alex into a tight embrace. He kissed him deeply and couldn't contain his joy.

"You don't know how happy this makes me. We're going to have so much fun working together!"

"Not so fast, buster! I need a break before I start working on another cookbook. And besides, if we are working together, we'll have to be professional. No nookie in the office!"

Nick deflated, "What? You mean, I can't do this any more?" and immediately started sucking a giant hickey on Alex's neck.

"Hey, I'm pretty sure that's sexual harassment in the workplace!" Alex giggled.

"You haven't signed anything yet!" Nick growled playfully, and returned to kissing him hard.

"Do you kiss all your business partners like that?"

"Only you, babe. Only you."

Nick slapped Alex playfully on the behind, making him yelp and burst out laughing. The two men headed out of the conference room toward the lifts.

"You know," Alex said with a hint of a tease in his voice, "If I start making all these healthy cupcakes, I might just waste away to nothing. Then what will you hold onto in bed?"

Nick froze on the spot, as if he hadn't considered that. While he obviously would never object to Alex losing weight, whether it be for health reasons or because he wanted to improve his level of fitness, he had to admit he would miss the soft, beautiful curves of Alex's body. That sweet belly and that gorgeous, cushioned round ass. But regardless of whether his boy was thin or thick, he would love him nonetheless. Alex was his everything.

Nick was snapped out of his inner thoughts by the sound of laughter. Alex had continued walking toward the lifts without him, cackling wildly. By the time Nick realised what was happening, Alex had dashed into the lift, the doors closing behind him, and the lift car had started it's descent to the ground floor. All Nick could hear was Alex giggling all the way down.

Nick chuckled to himself, shaking his head, then playfully chased after his boy. He headed for the other lift and pressed the call button impatiently, desperate to catch up.

Nick figured he'd never be done chasing the cupcake boy.

THE END

Don't miss out!

Visit the website below and you can sign up to receive emails whenever Alex Leslie publishes a new book. There's no charge and no obligation.

https://books2read.com/r/B-A-CCJI-SZSZ

BOOKS 2 READ

Connecting independent readers to independent writers.

About the Author

Alex Leslie is an Australian-born author of Gay M/M romance works including *Chasing The Cupcake Boy, Following His Bliss* and *My Big Gay Family Christmas Fiasco.*

Alex lives with his partner, two troublesome cats (who love sleeping on his laptop!) and is currently dealing with an ongoing addiction to iced coffee drinks.

Read more at www.alexleslieauthor.com.